VISITING ELSEWHERE

Anthology of Award-winning Short Stories

ISBN-13: 978-0-9742652-3-0
ISBN-10: 0-9742652-3-3

DEDICATION

This anthology is dedicated to those who tour "Elsewhere" daily

To the authors featured in this book: Scribes Valley thanks you for your time, patience, trust, and talent.

CONTENTS

TOURING ELSEWHERE
A Foreword by David L. Repsher, editor

Hi, there! I hope you're enjoying your stay here in Elsewhere. I'm sure you're finding all kinds of fascinating things to stimulate your imagination and emotions. Isn't it amazing how written words can transport you to faraway places? And not only faraway! They can transport you to places as near to you as...well...your own body—and that's pretty close!

Please forgive me for interrupting your visitation. I just wanted to make sure you're having a good time here and exercising your imagination to its fullest. Oops, sorry, my mistake. Your imagination is infinite so there's no way to exercise it to its fullest.

The stories you are about to encounter will give it a good shot, though. Let them attempt to fill your mind, and send your imagination reeling. Let them carry you away. Let them lead you further and further into...

ELSEWHERE

FIRST PLACE

THE TRAFFIC LIGHT
©2011 by Justin Carlton

In just a moment of life, one can live a lifetime. It is a testament to the power of the mind, the strength of the soul, and the weakness of the body. The body cannot continue where the physical parts ways with the spiritual. It is a battered and lonely kite suspended in the winds of time.

I am sitting at the traffic light, waiting for it to turn green.

Cars whiz by in either direction, unrestricted by time or space. They are mere entities: meaningless, shapeless, and indistinct—blurs my eyes cannot track. The intersection is a neon and concrete cocoon, the crossroads of a generation consumed with consumption, and another that simply didn't care.

My body is dragging, my eyelids are heavy. My flesh hangs like wash on a line, weary and loose and boneless. In this moment of time, this bare instant of my life, nothing matters to me but the traffic light. Obviously, it is refusing to change, but why? I want to go, I want to run. I want to shed the somnolent skin I wear and sprint through the driving rain, naked and formless and *alive*.

The sound of a horn penetrates my muffled consciousness. Behind me or in front of me, it doesn't matter: the sound is all-encompassing, eternal, *inside* of me. My senses are bleeding together in synesthesia. I can feel and hear and taste the shrill echoes all at the same time, and they consume me. The car vibrates with the swelling explosion of enraged noise.

As a boy, I might have been intrigued. I might have run my fingers over the trembling polyester seats and relished the tingling sensation that traveled almost painfully up my spine, jumping like an electric current. I might have found some aspect of pleasure within this sensorial phenomenon. The carnal, investigatory spirit of youth would have had me simultaneously thrilled and terrified. Now, although I cannot ignore the growing rumble, I can only wonder.

What is happening? Why am I waiting?

Why won't the light go green?

Without warning, remembrance stings my brain, alerting me to the fact that I simply don't have time, that I'm going to be desperately late. Panic straightens my spine rigidly, like a tombstone, and I grip the wheel with renewed strength. An inexplicable rush of adrenaline sets my heart pounding. I need to move, move, move, move, *move*—

But I cannot. The light has not gone green. It glares at me through the rain, angry and red and swollen. And so I wait, because I am powerless to do anything else.

Breathing shallowly, I watch the lightning–fast cars crisscross paths before me, wondering what exactly is so important— wondering what is so goddamn important to *any*one, them or me. Where are they going? Where was *I* going? Why was I rushing in the first place?

I am...

What?

Whom?

Where?

And why. Why won't the light change? Why does it *refuse* to go green?

This sudden amnesia is complete and debilitating. Terrifying. Had I the strength, I might have pounded on the wheel, blown the horn, cursed at the passersby—anything for release. But I have no energy, and with no capacity to change or to act, I possess no being. I am static. I exist on a substandard plain, below physical capacity, possessed of irrational thought. The powerlessness to act and to move is the most frightening thing. The sense of utter dependency on fate produces fear like I have never felt. Like punching under water, like running in dreams: you accomplish nothing, you move nowhere, and you cannot escape.

Helplessness.

"No," I mutter.

"Honey, when are you going to fix the shelf?"

"When I feel like it," I reply in a singsong sort of voice, allowing the minor aggravation I feel to mix with the feigned annoyance. Vaguely, I recall having this conversation before in a similar manner. It seems the same arguments tend to repeat over time, just the way history snobbishly likes to retell itself.

Behind me from the kitchen, in a voice full of mock anger: "Well, I feel like it, so that should be enough for you."

This is my wife: beautiful and loving, only two inches shorter than me, but far smarter and stronger—at least on the emotional plane. Italian, but without the accent or the tendencies, she is a phenomenal cook and loving mother to our son and daughter. She tolerates my love of tinkering, my wasted afternoons in front of the TV. Her only vice is chocolate, her only fault that she is too trusting.

She comes into the room, leans over the back of my chair, and plants a kiss on my temple, simultaneously pushing away the newspaper with a hand clad in an oven mitt gauntlet. "I love you even when you're nasty," she says close to my ear.

Of course, my exasperation melts with mixed guilt and affection. She has a knack for coercion. But who is this woman who loves me—even when I'm nasty? I cannot remember her name. Only her face.

Tears are suddenly in my eyes, falling hot on my cheeks,

distorting the angry red eye of the traffic light suspended in midair before the car.

What is *wrong* with me?

"Dad, can you help me with my homework?"

This is my son: small, young, but intelligent. Tolerates the bullying of the jocks without complaint. He is more mature than I was at his age, perhaps not my intellectual equal, but certainly better prepared for the world. He is obsessed with videogames, knows more about electronics and calculus than I ever will, is closer with his sister than I ever was with my only sibling.

"Sure," I say. "What do you need help with?"

"An essay." He drops awkwardly into the armchair across from me, clearing his throat to read from his textbook. English: his Achilles' heel. How ironic that he is reading Homer.

"He wants you to write it for him," his sister taunts, somewhere behind me.

This is my daughter: nineteen, single, strong like her mother. Her beautiful, beautiful eyes are identical to my wife's. She is incurably sarcastic, stubborn but obedient, carefree yet compassionate, and a second mother to her younger brother. She lives at home, attending community college, working toward a degree in interior design.

Impossibly, their names have also slipped my mind. They mean everything to me. They are my offspring, my children. Yet despite the years, despite our closeness, despite the circumstances dictating our lives, I cannot remember their names. Who are they?

And who am I? Certainly not their father; certainly not a husband. How can I be? I am not home, I am not with them. I have no recollection, no thought, no nothing but a sense of devastating wrongness and the overwhelming desire to be whole again.

Was I searching? Was I working? Was I traveling? What would I find? Would I ever go home?

The car trembles beneath me. The blacktop seems to be moving—crawling and alive—although the vehicle remains stationary. The sky boils with clouds, heavy and dark, hanging low over the town. The wipers scrape the windshield, squealing in half–hearted protest, a sound that grates my teeth together painfully. The light is still red. And in the rearview mirror—

My eyelids flutter.

I am ten years old, swimming in the lake behind our old Victorian house in Connecticut, just down the steep hill from the expansive, split–rail porch. It is early fall, and the season promises to be exceptionally cold. The crisp evening air tastes of aluminum and woody ash, because the neighbors seem to be constantly sacrificing piles of rainbow leaves to Demeter, or whatever god of autumn they believe in.

The murky water is heavy around me, frigid and opaque: an uninviting host to an invading explorer. But my youthful heart is strong and undeterred within my chest. I open my eyes, relishing the chill of the water prickling inside my head, as if it had physically traveled through my pupils and sloshed into my brain. I am beneath the world, yet I am on top of it.

Something glimmers at the bottom of the lakebed, something that catches the refracted, dying sunlight and sparkles in the corner of my eye. A moment later it is gone, and I pause in mid–stroke, staring down into the darkness in an attempt to glimpse St. Elmo's fire once more. Clouds drift listlessly overhead and liquid sun spills over the muddy floor fifteen or more feet below me. And there it is again, glinting in a circle of grimy rocks, calling out to me: a child full of imagination, raised on adventure TV and picture books of sunken ships, dinosaur bones, and cowboys of the Wild West.

I dive.

The temperature drops with each foot. The pressure weighs heavily on my ears, squeezing my head almost painfully. I blink against the frigid water, pumping my arms and legs to reach the bottom. *It seems like forever before I can touch the slimy muck coating the creek bed, and then I crawl on numb fingers and toes towards the irregular ring of rocks where I had spied my treasure. My lungs are burning already, but I have come too far now to retreat.*

I hover over the bottom, searching for the prize. But there is nothing of interest in the mud—nothing but rocks and various assortments of litter, slowly decomposing with the years. And there it is: the glimmer, so enticing, shining deceptively from the ridged, circular spine of a bottle cap partially buried in the mire.

The first thing I feel is disappointment. I have not found treasure. I have found rubbish.

The second thing I feel is the pressure in my chest.

Suddenly I realize just how long I have been submerged, as if the absolute numbness in my extremities is not indicator enough. I invert my body and plant my feet on the muddy rocks, then propel myself up, up towards the distant sky. My legs and arms quickly grow weak with exertion as I frantically pull and kick at the water, desperate to reach air. I am moving but getting no closer. The dying sunlight is so very far away, and my limbs begin to fail me. I am utterly exhausted, powerless. The water holds me imprisoned, frozen in fluid medium. Everything begins to darken as I sink slowly back into the depths, one hand feebly outstretched toward the heavens.

Everything stops.

And then: a hand, rough and warm and strong, clasps mine.

The air slaps my face as I break through the surface, fresh and bitingly cold—colder by far than the water. My savior hauls me out of the water, and then I find the ground beneath my knees and hands. It is blessedly hard and firm, strong enough to support me. My fingers tighten reflexively around fistfuls of sickly grass, and I slump onto one shoulder, my face in the dirt and my butt in the air. The scent of cold, autumn soil fills my head as I gasp and choke for air, vomiting water from my lungs.

A shadow hovers anxiously over me.

This was my father: a man of ambition, always working, fatefully barred from success, forever angry—not with me and not with my mother, but unhappy despite our best efforts to please him. We love him; he loves us. It is a rule of thumb, but none of us show it exceptionally well. We are together but alone. We are one but many.

"Are you fucking stupid?!" he demands, grasping me painfully by the shoulders and lifting me from my penitent position. He roughly turns me around, setting my feet on the frigid earth, but I am too exhausted to hold myself erect. "Are you fucking stupid?!"

With my head lolling weakly on my shoulders, I glimpse the terror in his stare, the glassy sheen of tears glazing his ceramic eyes with their dilated pupils and spider–web veins. His rugged face is white. He almost lost me, and he knows it.

This is how I will always remember him. This is the moment that defines him to me forever.

Despite the fact that I am almost as tall as his chest, despite the fact that his arthritic back has ever given him trouble, he lifts me in his arms. Holding me tight, carrying my naked body as though it weighs nothing, he sprints for the big old house on the hill.

Life has a knack for being unbelievably ironic. History has this strange habit of repeating itself. Death has this odd power to be terrifying but beautiful at the same time. To some, these things are one and the same, parts of a whole. To others, a mystery. But to me, they are gifts of experience, temporarily permanent. We will taste them all.

My son is just born. He is barely seconds old.

"It's a boy," the doctor tells us, and I can see the smile in his eyes despite the fact that the blue surgical mask covers the lower half of his face. His weary voice is enthusiastic, tinged by relief that all has gone well with my wife's delivery. "It's a boy," he

repeats, for the benefit of my shock.

A boy. A son.

Mine. Ours.

The nurse holds him carefully, and I snip the umbilical cord with the doctor's aid, unable to take my eyes from the tiny crimson face, the tiny fingers curling and opening, the tiny mouth wide with the first cries of childhood.

As the doctors work to clean him, I return to my wife's side. I grip her feverish hand with both of my own, literally bouncing on the balls of my feet with excitement. She is too weary to show the same ecstatic joy, too weak, but I can see the life in her teary, bloodshot eyes. She smiles at me, and I cannot help but burst into joyful tears as I grin foolishly in return.

We have given life again. We have created. A son this time!

Would that my father was still alive—to see his grandson, to witness this miracle work of God. I know he would have been happy, perhaps for the first time in his life. I can imagine the joy on his face as he sees his grandson's face for the first time. He would have been enamored with the prospect of helping to raise my boy, and—in so doing—finally heal the wounds he had inflicted on the both of us.

In the next moment, there is a scream: a bloodcurdling screech of terror. My son, a pink bundle of flesh, life, and potential, slick with blood and fluids from the womb, slips from the nurse's hands and falls toward the floor.

The blood on the linoleum is not only my wife's.

Powerless, I cannot move, I cannot think, I cannot breathe. My wife is screaming, struggling to sit upright and fighting to get to our son, but she has no strength left in her body to rise, to pull herself from the bed. I don't remember letting go of her hand, I don't remember pushing the doctor away. But now I am on the floor, crashing to my knees and scooping up my broken son, cradling his broken head, and screaming broken sounds with no words.

The doctor is pulling me away as a nurse takes the limp body *from my arms and scrambles from the room, shouting orders to the others. The responsible nurse slumps against the wall, slides to the floor, almost as lifeless as my son, staring blankly at the bloody mess on the linoleum.*

"We're going to save him!" the doctor shouts in my ear, but I am fighting him, I am fighting for my son whom I have just met, who does not even have a name.

Yet. Yet.

He holds me tightly, shouting over my protests: "We will save your son—"

"Your daughter is okay, she's fine—she's fine. She's going to be alright. Please just take a seat and we'll be back to get you soon. Please just stay calm. She's going to be alright."

I hold my wife by the shoulders, fighting to keep her from following the gurney as the doctors whisk it down the hall towards the ER, shouting for the men and women in the hallway to move aside. The droplets of blood left behind on the floor are liquid pieces of our daughter's life, leaking away.

"What happened?" I demand, drawing my sobbing wife into an embrace. "What happened?"

"Accident," my wife gasps, grabbing fistfuls of my shirt and burying her face in my chest. "Head-on."

My daughter has only had her license for two months—barely enough time to practice, barely enough time to learn. She has been driving the old Toyota, which is technically still my wife's and mine, but we let her call it hers to impress her friends and to feel grown up. Her younger brother has declared her his permanent chauffer to chess club because she always lets him put the windows down while she drives.

But she has next to no experience on the road, and now maybe she never will.

Over the top of my wife's head, I watch with inexplicable fury as a nurse wearing latex gloves and a mask wipes up the blood from the hallway floor and then sprays an antiseptic to eliminate the germs. I want to scoop up that blood in a jar and save every last drop for my sweetheart—to return it to her. This man has no idea how much she means to me. He does not care that drops of my daughter are wasted. To him, those lost droplets can be replaced, recreated. They are expendable and it is part of life.

But to me, they are priceless.

They both lived. We *all* lived. I can remember neither details nor complications. But we lived, and in the end, that is all that matters.

Fate: the controlling factor, a force of God, an often supernatural extension of reality.

My daughter has never driven since the accident. She has no left breast and four of her ribs are artificial. My son has always had a speech impediment, has never had full use of his left arm, will have a permanent lazy eye until his death. My wife has been stricken with eternal paranoia since the car accident, has never fully trusted doctors since we nearly lost our boy, and is often subject to vivid nightmares.

Yet we are comparatively fortunate. Our family survived when countless others have crumbled. And through the suffering, we grew stronger. We *are* strong.

But who are they? And *who am I?*

The mystery goes unanswered.

I trace my eyes over the dashboard and the passenger side of the car. The haze of the afternoon storm clouds my eyes for a moment but then lifts again, like a window slowly clearing from the fog of someone's eager breath. My father is sitting in the passenger seat beside me, my mother behind me. In the rearview mirror, I can see that my estranged brother is beside her and a childhood friend is seated on his other side. All of them are smiling and waving, like at family reunions with barbecues and horseshoes where no one remembers anything about anyone else but vague details concerning careers and degrees. But they have all been dead for years—long and painful years. Have they been driving with me this whole time, waiting for the light along with me?

And suddenly, although I cannot remember much of anything, although I have no sense of self, my predicament has a meaning and a purpose. I am stopped beneath Jacob's ladder, before Charon's barge, just waiting for the green light.

Waiting to go.

There is only one thing keeping me here, only one thing sustaining my breaking lungs and failing heart, bidding them carry on. The blood pumping from my veins is a timekeeper: slowing, slowing, crawling, stopping, *freezing*. All as the moment nears.

It takes every last ounce of my strength to pull the handle and push open the door. The seatbelt keeps me from escaping. I fight it, finding the clasp and releasing it, so that I fall heavily from the cab to the asphalt. The pain in my hands and elbows is muted, distant. The rain instantly soaking my flesh is icy, but the blood on my face is hot. Is it mine? I crawl on my belly toward the sidewalk where all those faceless people stand. Several are coming toward me, maybe to help, screaming and shouting without meaning. Sound, not words. Noise, but not music.

Hands are pulling me toward the curb because I can't do it alone, lifting me by my arms, turning me over onto my back. The rain is pouring in my head and on my skin. Everything is going dark—inside and out. My head rolls lifelessly back on my shoulders, and I cannot lift it. I see the brooding sky, the faceless people upside–down, the flashing blue and red strobes, the lightning—

No...

My nameless family, my beloved wife and children. Why aren't they here? Where was I going—why was I ever leaving them? How can I bear to be away from the three people I love more than anything, who love *me* despite my flaws, even when I'm nasty? Have I always loved them the way I should?

Am I going to die alone?

Reality is cruel, a soulless mistress who hears no pleas—only reason. And I have no reason. I have no answers. But I have a heart and I have names. Remembrance, blissful and cooling, breaks the subconscious dam, filling my brain with the memories and the names I should never have forgotten. I can see their faces. I can see them smiling, reaching out for me across the distance that separates us. I can almost touch them. I can almost feel them near me.

My heart is swollen with love, yet it is slowing...slowing...s...l...o...w...i...n...g...

It is our wedding night. The summer air is heavy but comfortable, still cooling from the heat of the day. Crickets fill the stillness with their monotonous chorus, perhaps an attempt to give us the privacy a newly wedded couple deserves on their first night as one. We're not listening, they say, and rub their wings together conspicuously, turning their hard little backs to the open window of our bedroom.

My wife puts her forehead to mine as we lie facing each other on the pillow. She is still breathing heavily from our recent exertion, looking into my eyes with such joy and adoration as I have never before experienced. I know I am smiling too, and I have been for a while, because my cheeks are aching pleasurably.

For some time, we merely lie that way, saying nothing. Words have passed beyond meaning. We have a language all our own now, something that surpasses verbal communication and body language, rendering any vain stab at explanation utterly meaningless.

People oversimplify. They reduce love to emotion and pessimism. In defining human nature, they define exactly what it is not. The beauty of the soul is the little boy's shadow, which he will attempt to pin with his foot to the sidewalk. The dog will chase its tail, the poet will force his muse, but in the end, there is nothing under heaven that can truly be defined with words. And if there was something that plain, that basic and primitive, would it really be worth describing in the first place?

"You're so close," my wife whispers softly, searching my eyes with an understanding no one else could possibly possess. She finds my hand and pulls it to her lips.

"You are too," I say, dragging a finger across her cheek.

As we fall asleep together, I find myself wondering how I have lived so long without this connection to another human being. I think of the past and the future, but mostly of now: the bed where we lie, the lazy hum of the ceiling fan, my wife breathing softly against my chest. I never want to leave this place, this sanctuary.

I have tasted heaven, and I know I can never be alone again.

And I am not alone.

Just before I fall into darkness, my eyes focus for one last moment, past the steaming wreckage of my car and the twisted hulk of the truck that hit me from behind, through the thickening sheets of falling rain, and onto the traffic light, silhouetted against the sky.

And the light goes green.

About the author:

Logically, writing his author's bio should be easier than writing the actual story, but sadly this is not the case. Justin finds himself torn between writing about his less-than-illustrious career as a writer (if melodramatic fiction from the pen of a 21-year-old English student can count as such) and his passion for writing and performing music. In a nutshell, Justin has been writing fiction since he was old enough to string words together and writing/performing music since he could strum a guitar. Justin likes to spend his time reading all genres of literature, cartooning, playing soccer, and rooting for his Phillies. Most importantly, he is a Christian whose faith in God is not some type of superficial means of assuring himself of eternal destiny, but based on an intimate relationship with his Savior, Jesus Christ. Finally, Justin would be remiss if he didn't thank his parents and close friends who have encouraged and supported him in his artistic endeavors, and he hopes to build upon this, his first published work, and continue to make them proud in the future. It is an honor that someone, anyone out there, is reading this now.

SECOND PLACE

CHICKEN HEAD
©2011 by Michelle Wotowiec

At twenty-four years old, I still feel ashamed walking through the glass doors of the clinic. Inside, the windows are plastered with black tape, promising privacy for those of us who need to keep our secrets. As I walk through the second set of doors and into the lobby, I see three young girls sitting in the misplaced cafeteria chairs off to my right. Each girl wears a baggy tee shirt, tight jeans, and large hoop earrings. They all stare blankly at the old tube television screen. A PBS program telling of how different colored vegetables help different parts of your body plays to the zombie audience. Across the room from the girls is a man in his early twenties. He has shoulder length brown hair tucked behind his ears. He wears a bleach-stained button up shirt and jeans with ripped knees. A little girl, dressed up like a doll in pink lace, with cheeks blushed by tear stains, sits on his left knee.

I make my way to the receptionist shielded by the glass window. I offer a half smile as I wait for her to acknowledge me. The heavy seconds pass, however, and she does not look up from her desk. Watching her lips, she appears to be repeating the word "unacceptable" into the telephone receiver. I imagine turning around and walking out the way I came. No one is forcing me to go through this embarrassment, this humiliation.

As if reading my thoughts, the receptionist glances up and puts her pointer finger in the air as she turns her body to the side. Forty-five seconds later she stands up and opens the glass window, allowing our worlds to collide: "Your name?" She sounds pleasant, but her cheeks are pink with frustration.

"Madison," I manage to spit out.

"Your last name, Madison?"

"Weyerbacher" I look at the floor. "W-E-Y-E-R-B-A-C-H-E-R."

"And your date of birth?" She is no longer looking at me, but is looking at the sheet of appointments on the desk in front of her.

"Twelve twenty-eight eighty-five."

She fumbles through some papers, and clips three sheets to a clipboard. "Here, fill these out and bring them back."

I take the clipboard from her hands and carry it over to a chair near the man and his baby. The doll baby looks at me while the man pretends to watch the PBS program. Her eyes, dishwater blue, are unforgiving—accusing, even. I want to tell the man to turn his baby's head away from me; to make her stop tearing my skin off my bones, leaving me raw.

I fill in my name, my date of birth, my address, my phone number, my e-mail, I check the uninsured box, and begin to read through the long lists of diseases that I have never had. After I fill out the first and second pages, I flip to the third, which has a title of *Sexual Intercourse History*. I feel a knot form in my throat as I read through the questions and fill in the blanks:

ARE YOU SEXUALLY ACTIVE?
Yes

WHEN WAS YOUR LAST INTERCOURSE?
+/- Two weeks ago

DO YOU PRACTICE SAFE SEX?
Yes

WHAT METHOD?
The pill

HOW LONG HAVE YOU BEEN WITH YOUR CURRENT
PARTNER?
Two years

DO YOU PRACTICE VAGINAL SEX?
Yes

DO YOU PRACTICE ORAL SEX?
Yes

DO YOU PRACTICE ANAL SEX?
No

DOES YOUR PARTNER CURRENTLY HAVE OR HAS EVER HAD
ANY STDS THAT YOU ARE AWARE OF?
No

HOW OLD WERE YOU WHEN YOU FIRST HAD SEXUAL
INTERCOURSE?

At this question, my hand freezes. Do I tell the truth? Does it really make a difference at what age I began having sex? I feel the heavy pen between my fingertips and close my eyes.

I first entered this same clinic at the age of fifteen. My sister had dropped me and my boyfriend, Lance, off on her way to basketball practice. I wore an oversized Nirvana hoodie and baggy pants, Lance wore a white tee shirt and straight-legged blue jeans. I hid my face behind my bleach blonde hair. His hand was placed on my thigh for what felt like an eternity. Lance was a year older than me. We had sex within the first two weeks of being exclusive, but at that point we had been dating for about four months. Until that afternoon, sitting in the clinic draped in my Nirvana hoodie, I was pretty sure I loved him. Then again, I thought I loved almost every guy I slept with. I was young, but never felt the youngness in my bones until I sat in this very lobby with Lance nine years ago as I waited for some reaper to call me into the back room. I remember the feeling in my stomach and how badly I wanted Lance to take his hand off my thigh. I felt dirty. Greasy. Nuclear. I didn't want to be touched. I hated Lance. We sat in the room for twenty-five minutes in silence before a lady with curly blonde hair wearing a white jacket called me back.

"Are you fully aware of what you are doing?" she asked politely as she sat across from me in an oversized chair with a clipboard in her hand.

"Yes," I managed to respond.

"You read the packet before you signed it?" She looked me in the eye, trying to catch my lies.

I nodded my head.

"Okay, take this as soon as possible. You will need to eat something with it." She placed the clipboard on the desk and stood up out of her chair. I felt the disappointment in her voice—or at least I thought I did.

Again, I nodded my head.

"Pay the receptionist the thirty-five dollars on your way out."

I stood from my own chair, my body feeling like barbed wire as I made my way back out the door and to the receptionist's desk. I paid her the money and walked right past Lance and to the shoddy parking lot. I stood in the rain, waiting for him to catch up. Lance and I crossed the street with cement feet and made our way over to Burger King. I remember the weight of the water in my hair and way Lance kept licking the rain from his lips. Once inside, he bought me a cheeseburger, fries, and a small Diet Coke. We sat at a booth, neither saying a word as I placed the pill on my tongue and sipped the Diet Coke. After the pill was in me, I remember feeling amazed at just how easy it was. One slip up, one broken condom, could be fixed so easily. All it cost was thirty-five dollars, a cheeseburger, a fry, and a Diet Coke.

As this thought passed through my brain, I felt alien. I felt inhuman. I mean, it only happened the night before, and it was only a pill but...but something felt wrong. Or illiterate. Immature, maybe.

When I finally had the nerve to look at Lance, I began to cry. Not uncontrollably, but salty tears streamed down my cheeks and into my mouth. I turned my face to the side, looking at anything but Lance, wanting to hide the unexpected weakness. He came over to my side of the booth and sat next to me. He placed his hand on my thigh again, trying to let me feel his support through his touch, but neither of us was able to look at the other. How was I supposed to ever look at him again without tasting the pill on my tongue? Cliché? Sure.

I look at the question on the paper in front of me again:

HOW OLD WERE YOU WHEN YOU FIRST HAD INTERCOURSE?

I am not a little girl anymore. I am twenty-four years old. I am not a little girl anymore. I am not a little girl anymore. Yeah, I started young. Yeah, I knew I shouldn't have been doing it. Sure, I can try to blame it on MTV and all of the sluts of Hollywood. But in my gut, I still hear all of the conservative old women with red lips gasping at the thought, deciding I would never amount to anything. My right hand involuntarily writes the response to the question:

13

I look at the number written in ink and it feels foreign. Unfamiliar. Unfair. This number is only a number when written on paper, but in my stomach, it is a worm eating away my insides. Today, sitting in this room, having written it on this sheet of paper, thirteen is so young. *Too* young. But honestly, at the time, I didn't feel so young. I felt every cell in my body. I was so...*alive*. I almost had sex when I was twelve, but (ironically) decided I wasn't ready. So, making it until thirteen didn't really seem so bad. He was a redhead and, sad to say, he was sixteen. At thirteen years old, there is little difference between being a thirteen-year-old girl and a sixteen-year-old boy. Now, looking back as a twenty-four-year-old woman, my stomach hurts. He should have...I don't know. He shouldn't have.

That wasn't Lance, though. Lance was later.

I look down to the next question:

HOW MANY SEXUAL PARTNERS HAVE YOU HAD?

Again, I hesitate. These women, they'll judge me. They're doctors, I know, but I hate spilling my secrets on paper. I don't want to write down the number.

Oh, I know the number; the number is engraved in my brain like a tumor. I carry it with me every second of every day, but I can't picture all of their faces, these boys...men. Some of them, I really cannot place their eyes, nose, mouths, freckles...they have become the distorted, clichéd face of a mistake.

One of the girls gets up and walks through the door to the back after her name is called. Pregnancy test? Maybe. STD test? Maybe. It couldn't be for the morning after pill, though, because they don't make you wait this long.

I take the pen back into my hand and write my number onto the paper for the world to see:

11

There. I think about my first time. I was thirteen and was so in love with that guy. I was the butterflies, the hiccups, the goose bumps, the whole nine yards. Jeff with his fire-red hair and powder blue eyes; the way his touch ignited my skin. We didn't get naked. In fact, he didn't even take my pants completely off. He pulled them down to my ankles, lifted my legs up, and slid in. The pain, which united me with every other woman who went through the experience, was anything but orgasmic. But, of course, it was a child's love and I fell out after only ten months. I remember the way he cried when I'd moved on—at sixteen years old he cried like a child—and begged me to stay, to run away with him, to marry him. I remember how badly he scared me with this declaration and remember the wounds on his wrists that he flaunted through his tears. What was he doing now? Was he still having sex with girls with pants around their ankles? Was he a father? A husband? Alive?

The second was even more intense, surprisingly, and the one who is still able to make my stomach flip, but not for the right reasons. We dated on and off for years. If my life was a fairytale, I would have ended up with him. I loved him a way I had never loved anyone before. But life is not a fairytale and I grew up. Like the rest, his face is disappearing as the time passes.

The third was a drunken mistake. The fourth was my best friend. The fifth was Lance. The sixth was a guy who dropped a lot of acid. The seventh was a singer in a band. The eighth was a friend of a friend of a friend and was only the one night. The ninth wanted nothing but what he got. And the tenth...well, he fell for his bassist.

How's that for vague? Time not only sweeps away the minor details but sucks up all of those intimate moments as well. I remember very few, today, looking back at my eleven. I remember the first by default and the second because it really was love. But the rest, well, it's basically like hearing someone else's story. I can't remember how my skin felt when they touched it or how their lips tasted against mine.

Eleven? He is current. We live together, unmarried, in a one-bedroom apartment with two cats. We eat Thai food on Thursdays, Olive Garden on Tuesdays, and watch a lot of movies together on our sectional couch. We wash each other's hair and sing each other songs. Love is love and he and I have found something comfortable.

I can't write all of this on the paper on my lap. I can't try to justify my promiscuity in describing my own happy ending. But I write the number down anyway. I write it because I'm twenty-four years old and I have no other choice.

I finish the questionnaire and return it to the lady through the glass window.

An hour later, a thin lady with curly blonde hair, wearing a white coat, calls my name and leads me to the back room. The room looks just as it did nine years ago and for a moment I wonder if the lady remembers my face.

"First thing, Madison, I am going to need you to stand on the scale." She points to the scale and I cling my purse, packed full with my netbook, *The Mammary Plays, An Autobiography of Red,* and *Welcome to Elsewhere,* to my side.

108. She seems satisfied and scribbles the number into her notebook.

"Have a seat. I am going to have to ask you a few questions." She taps her pen against the desk while she looks over the paper that displays my past mistakes in the form of numerical numbers. "Okay, well, let's start with when was your last menstrual cycle?"

"Sunday. I started Sunday." I had started Sunday, I clearly remember serving table 33 their Cokes when the cramp set in that sent me heading for the box of tampons in my car.

"And your periods are...normal?" She looks up from her paper.

"Yes."

She seems happy with this response and again scribbles in her notebook. I see the same picture of Abraham Lincoln, in his tall black hat, that I saw sitting in this room at fifteen years old. It seems as if this place stopped time while I was away and only continued running upon my return, like a jack-in-the-box. It only plays when the top is open. I am the controller of the jack-in-the-box-clinic.

"Would you consider taking an HIV test?"

"What?" I spit out, involuntarily.

"Well, Madison, it might be a good idea if you take an HIV test.

Not that there is any reason to worry, it is just a precaution."

"I don't...I don't have HIV. I couldn't possibly." My throat burns like bare skin on hot asphalt.

"Have you been tested before?"

"Well, no—"

"And do you know each of your partner's history of sexual intercourse?" She scratches her nose as she waits for my response.

No. I mean, some of them were virgins. At least that is what they told me—but not all of them. The band guy, specifically, he could have been with...fuck, he could have been with anyone for all I knew. He was almost ten years older than I was. He had a kid, he was a singer in a band...what else did I know about him? The others I knew. We were all from a small town and sex lives spread pretty quick in small towns.

"No. I don't know all of that," I say in almost a whisper.

"Would you be willing to take an HIV test?"

"When?"

"Now. Right now."

"Right now?"

"Yes, right now."

"Well, what do you do? What do I do?"

"It's a simple prick. I will prick your finger and put your blood on this test strip."

When I woke up this morning, the last thing I expected was to get tested for HIV. And worse even, I had never even considered the possibility of having HIV. Sex was sex and it was usually a mistake, but it wasn't deadly. It couldn't be deadly. Me and Kyle, the band guy, we used a condom. *Did* we use a condom? I don't know. I mean, I was drunk a few times and it all happened so...and I was always on the pill.

"Will you take the test?" she asks again, growing stern.

"O—Okay. I mean, if you think I should, I will." My eleven flash through my mind like a home movie. I try to remember little details, maybe ex-girlfriends mentioned in passing. Had they all told me how many girls they'd been with? My entire body begins to throb. My knees ache and my toes go numb.

She opens the drawer to her right and pulls out a needle and a clean test strip. "I just need your finger," she says, almost sweetly.

I involuntarily put my left pointer finger onto the table.

"Relax your arm."

I try to stretch my arm out so it will appear to be relaxed. But how can she expect me to relax? This lady, who apparently does not remember me from nine years ago, has just turned my entire world upside down. I feel beads of sweat form all along my hairline and my heart beats rapidly in my chest. I have never felt so inside my own skin.

She cleans my finger with sanitizer. "Are your hands always this cold?"

No, my hands are not always this cold. My entire body is reacting to those letters: HIV.

"Okay, you're going to feel a big prick." At that she presses the needle into my finger. I barely feel it and then she is placing the syringe back in the plastic bag. A little bubble of blood surfaces. "Here, bring your arm below your heart so I can get a little more blood." She leads my arm off of the desk and brings it down toward my lap.

She collects the blood she needs on the test stick, sets the test stick aside on the desk, and continues to ask me questions about my family's medical history. She tells me to take off my pants, underwear, and bra after she leaves the room. I can place the paper blanket over my lap. The doctor will come in just a few minutes. She takes the test stick with her but leaves the clipboard behind for the doctor to see.

I undress more quickly than I ever have before. I kick off my black and white high heels and rip off my pants and underwear. My entire body shaking, I pull my arms through the sleeves of my polka dot blouse and remove my bra. In nothing but my blouse, I pull myself onto the examination bed and cover my lower half with the stiff paper blanket. And I wait.

There is a knock on the door. "May I come in?"

I wait. I don't think I really want her to come in. I think I have had enough for the afternoon and would like to get dressed, walk back through the lobby and out the glass doors. I want to leave this alternate universe I have slipped into. I want to erase the letters HIV from the pores of my skin.

Another knock. "Madison?" She cracks the door and peeks through. "Are you decent?"

Ha, the irony. "Ye—yeah, you can come in. Sorry."

Doctor Horowitz is a plump woman in her late forties, early fifties. Her cheeks are pink and her smile is real. I like her. My body instantly loosens and I begin to feel the blood return to my veins.

"How are you, Madison?" She holds her hand out for me to shake.

"I'm good, thanks." I give a half smile in return and shake her hand.

"So, what brings you here today?" She picks up my clipboard from the desk to our left.

"Well, I am on my last packet of birth control, it's been a year since my last pap test, and—"

"Ah, so you're here because you have to be? Not because you're sick or—"

"Right. I just need more birth control." I smile, making eye contact. She eyes my chart and as she turns to the third page I feel a slight pain in my stomach. Again, I want to melt to the floor as another stranger sees the history of my sexual intercourse in the form of numerical numbers. I try to watch for a look of disgust to envelope her face as she devours the contents of the page.

Instead, she says nothing. She eyes the page quickly, taking mental notes and wheels her chair next to me on the examination bed.

"So, let's just get to it, shall we?"

"Okay," I say shyly.

"Are you currently sexually active?" Her hand is on her chin, her elbow on the edge of the bed.

"Yes," I say confidently.

"And when was the last time you had intercourse?" she asks matter-of-factly.

"Umm...a little more than two weeks ago." I begin to chew on the skin around my left pinky nail.

"And does your partner treat you right?" Her face shows no expression as she looks me in the eyes.

I take my pinky out of my mouth. "Yes, of course. He's a good guy. A very good guy." And he is. I say this to her proudly, although I feel she asked me this question based on my numbers on the clipboard. I know very well that a high number of sexual partners can be a warning sign to other things—bigger things. Promiscuous girls often end up with terribly abusive partners; promiscuous girls are often sexually molested as children, and so on. I, though, am none of those. I am not the stereotype. I had sex young out of curiosity, and I just continued doing it. None of my eleven ever laid a finger on me that I did not want at the time and none of them ever hurt me...physically.

"Good. I'm glad to hear it. I only ask because...well, I ask everyone that. It's important to be in a healthy relationship." She stands off her chair and picks up a pair of gloves from the desk drawer. "Do you ever examine your breasts on your own time?" She starts to pull up my blouse, but it snags on my navel ring. "Ooh, sorry about that. Are you okay?"

"Yes, I'm okay. And yes, I do my own checks." I lie on my back with my eyes closed, not sure of what to think about. Should I think about my own breasts, or of Dr. Horowitz and how close she feels to me right now, as if she is overstepping a boundary set by my body? And what about that test stick? Where did the nurse take it? Does Dr. Horowitz know that I am being tested for HIV?

"Okay, everything feels just fine." She takes her hands off my breasts. "Now I need you to scooch forward and place your feet on the stirrups."

I do as she instructs. She sits on the chair at the end of the bed and all I can see is the top of her head peeking above my paper blanket.

"You're going to feel a cold sensation." She is now in doctor mode, speaking to me as she does each of her patients and I feel relieved. The intimacy only a few minutes prior was overwhelming. "Now if this pinches, you tell me. I don't want to hurt you."

I feel a cold lubricant in my vagina and, again, I am not sure what it is I should think about. I close my eyes, erasing the top of her head from my mind and I think about my eleven.

Eleven. For the first time—maybe ever—I wonder what each of them is doing at this exact moment. I wonder whether they are happy. I wonder whether they count me the way I count them. I think about the band guy and how we had our first date at a coffee shop, but I didn't even like coffee. I drank it anyway, to impress him. He told me he had a five-year-old daughter. He told me that he was never really with the mother, but they had shared custody. He asked me how old I was. I told him nineteen, and he smiled. The conversation became flirtier and flirtier as the time ticked away. He rubbed his leg against mine under the table and I was so attracted to him: his dark hair, dark complexion, full beard, *green* green eyes. He was gorgeous and was interested in me. Right as we were about to leave—we were at my car—and right as I thought he was about to kiss me goodbye, he asked if he could see my driver's license. In a nice way, he said a girl tried to get with him once but she turned out to be only seventeen and he didn't want to ever get wrapped up in all of that again.

You know, if it were today, say, if I was in that coffee shop with Kyle right this minute, I would have laughed at him and told him to have a nice life, never to see him again. But that didn't happen today and I was young—even at nineteen I was young—so I showed him my ID. He looked at the birth date, looked at the picture, looked back at me, and then back at the picture. Finally, he shook his head in approval. We had sex five or six times in the following three or four weeks. Each time, I drove the forty-five-minute drive to his place and each time, I left before his daughter woke up at 8 am.

"All done. Now, that wasn't so bad, was it?" she says as she pulls off her rubber gloves.

"No, not at all," I respond as I open my eyes, reentering the room, allowing Kyle to disintegrate into thin air once again.

The doctor leaves the room so I can dress. I sit on the examination bed under my paper blanket and just breathe. I try to breathe my numbers through my lungs and exhale them into the air of the examination room. I need the numbers to lose power. I need them to lose meaning and release me. I get off the bed and step on the scale, in nothing but my blouse. 102. I'm not sure what the number means, or if it really means anything, as I snap on my bra, button up my blouse, pull up my pants, and place my feet back into my black and white heels.

I open the door and find Dr. Horowitz waiting for me in the hallway with the paperwork.

"Okay, Madison, I have ten packets for you. That should get you through...February. Now, you will have five additional packets you can pick up at any time between now and this time next year. But make sure they always give you at least three packets, because it's hardly worth the hour wait if not."

"Thank you." I shake her hand and she turns down the hall. I begin to cross the hallway to enter back into the lobby when the nurse with the curly blonde hair and white jacket calls from behind me.

"Madison, can you wait just a minute?"

My stomach climbs to my throat and I think I must have croaked a *yes* in response because she opens the door to the examination room back up and sits down at her desk. I see she is looking at the chair where she had me sitting less than an hour ago, telling me to relax. Again, I sit in it. I let the chair engulf my body.

Her face looks concerned and her eyes rip me right out of my skin. "Madison, I got your test results—" She fumbles through a few papers.

My test results? So soon? She can, they can—the test takes less than an hour? I look at her face and I close my eyes. I try to picture Kyle's face, or his daughters face, or anything—knowing that if it were positive, it was him who passed it. The guy I slept with while I was drunk, he was a virgin. We were both sixteen and ended up dating for seven or eight months afterward. The others, we were all from such a small town. Secrets didn't keep in our town and neither did sex partners. Kyle. It had to have been Kyle. How could I have been so—?

"The test came back negative."

"I—" My eyes begin to burn and I feel tears sliding down my cheeks, down my jaw. I begin to stand up, not understanding why she had to tell me that way, why she had to put me through the entire ordeal and not just saying *Hey, you don't have HIV!* And at the same time, I had never felt so alive, so outside of myself. In control of myself.

"Wait—" She places her hand on my shoulder. "Take this pamphlet with you anyway. It just gives all the facts. You know, how you can contract it and how to prevent it. You know, just look it over. It's always better to be safe than sorry."

I wipe the tears from my face and take the pamphlet from her hands. *HIV: What You Need to Know.* I stick it in my purse, between *The Mammary Plays* and my netbook. I thank her and walk back into the lobby. The girls are gone, as is the man and his baby. Now there is a new flock of girls sitting in the uncomfortable chairs with their palms on their thighs. On the left wall I notice a printed flier: *Free HIV testing every second Tuesday of the month.*

I turn from the children in the waiting room and walk through the glass doors, into the sunlight shining on the shoddy parking lot.

About the Author:

Michelle is an English Creative Writing graduate student at Cleveland State University. She has put together a collection of stories titled *We are the Skyscrapers* which she is avidly seeking publication. "Chicken Head" is included in the collection.

Michelle has been given honorable mention twice from Glimmer Train and my short story collection was a finalist in Grace Notes Publishing's 2010 competition. Her undergraduate writing portfolio at Kent State University received 2nd place in the Donna Zurava Memorial Prize competition. Michelle's story "Chicken Head" has been awarded 53rd place in the Memoirs/Personal Essay category of the 79th Annual *Writer's Digest* Writing Competition

She is an avid believer in writing from your gut and loving what you write.

She'd like to thank friends and family for all of their support in her writing endeavors.

She is honored to be published by Scribes Valley two years in a row.

THIRD PLACE

PUSH 'N SHOVE
©2011 by Ronna L. Edelstein

"Shit!" Vera shouts as the hot water scalds her back. Even though she has lived in the townhouse for three years, she still cannot remember which faucet controls which temperature. Maybe she should follow Ma's example by labeling the faucets with black permanent marker. After all, she has devoted her life to mimicking Ma as a way to perhaps catch Ma's elusive approval.

Trying to ignore the shampoo stinging her eyes, Vera blindly gropes for the correct faucet. Once she creates the perfect hot/cold balance, she stands under the spray, luxuriating in its tropical rainforest mist. She places a wet washcloth over her eyes, not only to ease the shampoo irritation but to block out gifts from the previous tenants: the water marks staining the beige tile, the chipped soap dish, and the discolored floor that no amount of cleanser can fix.

Instead of saving the hot water for Sarah and Peter, her teenage children, Vera turns up the pressure. She runs her soapy hands over her body, imagining a man someday doing this to her. Even when married, Vera did not receive watery caresses. Now, three years into her divorce, she doubts she ever will. Her fingers dance across her stomach, jumping over the vertical scar that begins at her belly button and disappears into her pubic hair. Five years ago, the hysterectomy not only deprived Vera of her reproductive organs, but also squelched any chance of survival for her marriage. The so-called husband rarely visited her during her initial hospitalization and two subsequent admissions due to infections. He also chose not to help with the kids or housework. Always a passive man, he withdrew more and more into himself, leaving Vera no choice but to hire a lawyer and file for divorce.

As the water turns lukewarm, Vera creates circles on her stomach, following the pattern taught to her by a Lamaze teacher as a way to ease tension. She feels herself relax as she enlarges the circles to include both breasts. Her fingers continue to move upward, encircling her neck and cupping her cheeks. Vera explores her body, delving into folds and crevices that only she has the right to touch. She feels her fingers tremble, as if the music of their dance has intensified. They long to massage that special spot—the one that makes Vera explode from the inside out—but Vera stops them. Today, of all days, she has no time for self-indulgence.

Instead, she soaps up the wash cloth and scrubs, even remembering to get behind her ears as Ma always insisted. She scrubs and rinses, rubs and...

"Oh, shit!" Vera shouts as her fingers collide with a lump. Vera tosses the wash cloth onto the tiled floor, re-explores the questionable area, and rediscovers the same lumpy spot. It is not like the benign lumps that led to four breast biopsies (two for each breast—as with shower water, Vera likes a balance), but it is a rock-like lump sitting atop the tip of her nose.

Vera roughly turns off the water, wraps a large blue towel around her somewhat chunky and sagging five foot eight inch body, and grabs a dry hand towel off the rack. Although she prefers the pain of the dentist's drill over the reality of her mirrored reflection, Vera now clears a spot on the steamy surface of the medicine cabinet mirror. She works carefully, intent upon creating the perfect Goldilocks spot that is big enough to reveal the thing growing from her nose, but small enough to hide her body.

Vera sees a mogul the color of week-old snow. It is huge, as if vials of growth hormones had been injected in it. It takes over Vera's face, shrinking her always bloated bottom lip and minimizing her beaver-like front teeth. It simultaneously mesmerizes and mortifies Vera.

"Shit, shit, shit!" Vera sways back and forth, hoping the motion will dislodge the lump. She wipes the rest of the mirror, grabs her glasses, and closely scrutinizes her nose through the middle section of her trifocals. The lump looms large, mocking her efforts to pretend it does not exist.

Careful to avoid her nose and its unwelcome visitor, Vera quickly dries herself and then puts on her grass-colored sweat suit, the one that turns her into the Jolly Green Giant. A pair of thick socks, once white but now pink after she accidentally washed them with a red shirt (Ma would never do that), gives her a Christmas-like appearance—an ironic picture considering her less-than-jolly "ho-ho-ho" mood. Vera tries to sneak downstairs without encountering either Sarah or Peter. But Sarah, hearing Vera's door open, marches out of her room in attack mode. Without turning around, Vera continues her descent from one level of hell into another.

"Ma, Peter is hogging the bathroom again. Why can't you do something about this?"

"Ma, tell Sarah that the more she pounds on the bathroom door, the longer I'm staying inside."

"Ma, this just is not fair!"

"Life's not fair, Sarah, so get used to it. And leave me alone!" As if to emphasize his words, Peter increases the pressure in his shower.

Vera stands mutely, wondering when her 16-year-old son and 14-year-old daughter became these alien creatures with no resemblance to their younger selves. She remembers when both begged for walkie-talkies as holiday gifts. "Then we can always talk to each other!" five-year-old Sarah had gushed. "Yeah, Ma, we can even talk when we're in our rooms asleep," Peter had added.

They used to spend hours together, performing plays that Peter wrote or turning Sarah's Barbies into distressed damsels who needed Peter's Star Wars figures to rescue them. They whispered together, Sarah's brownish-blonde curls brushing against Peter's darker, straighter hair. Sarah learned her Letter People from Peter; he taught her everything she needed to know to succeed in kindergarten.

Now, they have become monsters with serpent tongues and hearts of stone. Sometimes Vera imagines them as blobs—amorphous shapes distinguished only by gaping mouth-like holes. Words dripping venom spew from these mouths. Vera wonders whether the witch-like thing on her nose is a sign of the malignancy eroding her children and her life.

Letting Sarah and Peter resolve the bathroom battle, Vera trudges down the steps. She almost hopes she will fall like she did the year before. She had lain on the bottom step, lost in the pain of a concussion and a broken right foot. After making sure she still breathed, Peter had stepped over her prostrate body, headed for the kitchen, and then complained when he had found an insufficient supply of milk. Sarah, always good in an emergency, had called for help. Knowing that the divorce had imprisoned Peter in a hormonal household devoid of any male role model, Vera had never blamed her son for that moment of callous indifference. She had, however, blamed herself because, as Ma had taught her, the child's behavior reflects the teaching of the parent.

This time, however, Vera reaches the kitchen with no mishap. She has her usual breakfast of orange juice, a banana, and two handfuls of plain M & Ms. Munching on the candy, she presses her forehead against the kitchen window. The view looks as it always does: a lone tennis ball, probably Ted's from next door, lies against the curb; the first buds of spring peek out through the grass that borders the sidewalk; the initials that Sarah and her best friend carved into the newly laid-cement driveway still carry with them the "you're a bad mother" message (Ma would never have permitted the younger Vera to mar public or private property; she would never have permitted a Vera-like mogul to erupt on her nose).

"Ma, I need money for lunch. And remember, I'm staying late today for play rehearsal." Sarah, a budding thespian who has abandoned mundane speech for the more dramatic tones of a Shakespearean tragic heroine or an operatic diva, rushes into the kitchen.

Peter, racing behind her, grabs a bagel and begins his own tirade. "Ma, why do I have to drive Sarah to school? Why can't she take the bus like the other freshmen? Do I have to bring her home 'cause I have basketball practice and might want to hang out with the guys? And why does Sarah always think she can control the radio station?"

Vera, with her face still pressed against the window, wishes she could don an invisibility cloak. Instead, she speaks to the images of her children reflected in the glass.

"Peter, you will drive your sister to *and* from school. Sarah, you will get to choose the station going to school, and you, Peter, will choose coming home. And both of you will leave school pronto since Grandma and Grandpa are arriving today for their visit."

When she turns around to make sure she has clearly conveyed her message, she sees horror and derision, not the anticipated anger, on her children's faces.

"Ma, what is that thing on your nose? Gross! It's a good thing that you called off work today 'cause your sixth graders would really tease you about this."

"Yeah, Ma. Too bad it's not Halloween; you wouldn't even need a costume."

"Aren't you teaching *A Wrinkle in Time* now? You could be the real Mrs. Which!"

"Good one, Peter! Ma, your nose should be in *Ripley's Believe It Or Not*."

The teasing words sting Vera, but on this day she lacks the time and energy to retaliate with her own repertoire of biting words. Instead, she silently rejoices that her children can still find pleasure in one another, even if that pleasure turns her into their victim. Vera waves good-bye to Peter and Sarah, wishes them safe travels and a good day, and then does what she does every three months when Ma and Dad visit: rolls up her sleeves and begins the laborious task of turning the three bedroom, two-and-a-half bathroom townhouse into a pristine palace that Ma, the General of Cleanliness, will applaud. Vera knows, however, that she can dust, vacuum, mop, and spray, but not even a sterile house will earn kudos from Ma. On this day, especially, Ma will only have eyes for Vera's nose as if the plump pimple perching there represents all that is wrong with Vera. And yet Vera holds on to the miracle—the possibility that Ma will accept her, even if her house and body lack perfection.

Pulling at her upper lip, a nervous habit she developed when Ma used to coat her nails with some liver-like lotion to stop her from biting them, Vera heads into the dining room. She hates the massive table and even more bulky china closet, both souvenirs from her defunct marriage. Ma, famous for her push 'n shove cleaning style, would pull the china closet from the wall, making sure that no dust dared to dwell behind it. Vera, who has never been a push 'n shove housekeeper, hopes a volcano of dust lives there and, just as Ma walks by, will spew its dusty lava upon her. Maybe the screws holding the cushions in place on the dining room chair where Ma always sits will stage a mini-rebellion by loosening and imprisoning Ma in the empty space bordered by the four pieces of wood.

Vera turns on the vacuum, welcoming the machine's noisy breathing that drowns out her dastardly thoughts. She wants to be happy that her parents are driving the five hundred miles to see her, Peter, and Sarah, but Ma's critical attitude always messes up the reunion. As always, Ma will be too busy to even air-blow a kiss as she's dashing back and forth from the car to the house. Ma will lug in boxes of meals she has spent weeks preparing—a cooking spree not from love, but from a confirmed conviction that only *she* can provide sustenance to her at-risk grandchildren and inadequate daughter. Vera always sees Ma as a blur, as a woman whose hands, feet, and judgments are in constant motion. Only Dad, with his warm grin, kiss on her head, and hug, can give Vera a break, albeit a short one, from the indifference of her children, the strain of being a single parent, the evil interloper atop her nose, and the caustic comments of Ma.

"Can I help, Ma?" Vera knows she will greet Ma with these four words; she always does.

"Oh, no, dear, I'm sure you have other things to do." Vera knows Ma will give this response to Vera's desire to help; she always does.

Vera will then give a silent sigh, stand aside, and watch Ma rearrange the freezers; both the small one in the kitchen's refrigerator and the larger coffin-shaped one in the basement. Brisket with roasted potatoes. Kasha with bowed noodles. Spaghetti and casseroles, meatloaf and chicken. Cinnamon coffee cake and Toll House cookies. Peter and Sarah joke that without Grandma and pizza deliveries, they would starve. Vera laughs and eats with them, but she knows that some hungers cannot be sated with food.

Having completed the dining room and living room, Vera heads to the piano. When she was a little girl, Vera had begged for music lessons. Ma and Dad had signed her up for a violin class at the school, but even seven-year-old Vera knew that every tune she played wailed and whimpered like a dying cat. Grandma then bought her a piano, its wood the same hue as her favorite doll's blond hair. Vera took lessons taught by a talented neighbor, but the same fingers that skipped across a typewriter keyboard fumbled and faltered over the black and white piano keys. Ma stopped the lessons, refusing to squander any more money on Vera the musical failure. Years later, the then married Vera used her first paycheck as a part-time teacher to buy a piano—one whose wood was the rich cherry hue of promise.

Since the divorce, Vera rarely plays the piano. Peter, who can hear a song and perfectly play it, took lessons for a while, but he then decided basketball was a cooler way to spend his free time.

Sarah, who had learned how to read music in her vocal music classes, wanted to take piano lessons, but Vera, using language she had inherited from Ma, dismissed Sarah by snapping, "I don't have the extra money to waste on such an extravagance."

Vera fortifies herself with some low-fat yogurt and more handfuls of plain M & Ms before descending into the basement. She has not felt comfortable in a basement since Dad naively took her and her older brother to see *Psycho* when she was only thirteen. At the time, Vera's family lived in a house with a storage room under the steps. Vera knew Norman Bates's mother was rotting in that storage room, just as she knew Ma would send her there often to get a can of peas or a jar of applesauce for dinner.

The townhouse, thankfully, has a basement that is one large, open room. One corner holds the coffin-like freezer, another a village of boxes containing bits and pieces of her small family's lives. The washer and dryer sit in the third corner, while a hiccoughing water boiler dominates the fourth. Dad had hung a few clothes lines for Vera so she could air dry Peter's t-shirts ("Ma, put the hangar in through the bottom so the neck doesn't stretch") and Sarah's jeans ("No, Ma, I did not gain weight; you shrunk my jeans!").

Within ten minutes, Vera has not only swept the basement floor, but she has also stoically sacrificed Charlotte and her family to her cleaning mania. She checks the freezer one more time to make sure that room exists for the onslaught of food Ma will bring, and then she trudges up two flights of stairs to the second floor bedrooms and bathrooms.

Vera's room is not the problem. Her bedroom, vanity area (an oxymoron for a woman who hates mirrors and believes she has no feature about which to be vain), and bathroom always reflect the tidiness of the neurotically anal Vera. It is the kids' bathroom and bedrooms that present the problem. Because their bathroom has less emotional baggage than their bedrooms, Vera first enters the off-white room with its stained tiles. Bits of dried-up toothpaste dot the sink like acne on a teenager's face. As Vera rubs the toothpaste with cleanser, she remembers the Clearasil she once used to keep her then young face fresh and unmarked. Maybe she should buy some Clearasil for the pompous pimple. Or maybe she should just douse the pimple with cleanser.

With the sink and counters relatively clean, Vera attacks the tub. When she runs a brush down the drain, the bristles gather long strands of brown, blonde, and red hairs. Sarah likes to experiment not only with her hair color but also with her room. At least twice a week, Vera hears Sarah grunting and groaning as she pushes her bed from one wall to another, her desk from one corner to another, and her stereo to wherever. Every change in furniture involves a change in the arrangement of pictures hanging on the wall. Vera can only hope that should she ever move from the townhouse, she will have the patience to plug in all the empty holes so she can get back her security deposit.

Donning rubber gloves as if she is about to perform a colonoscopy on some ailing mammal, Vera tackles the toilet. As she sprays and wipes, rinses and flushes, Vera thinks about her diplomas—the *Summa Cum Laude* and Phi Beta Kappa ones from college, and the Master of Arts in Teaching one from graduate school—that lay in one of those basement boxes. Now she has a PhD in the Art of Toiletry, and a failing grade in "How to Please Ma 101."

Still, cleaning the commode is better than entering the kingdoms of her children. Vera debates the to-enter-or-not-to-enter question, but she senses that Peter and Sarah will better handle an invasion of their privacy than Ma will handle rooms that challenge her definition of ideal cleanliness. Although Vera hesitates, as if she can already feel the wrath of her children when they discover her sin, she knows that she has neither the time nor the patience to put off the inevitable. Vera needs to act—and she needs to act now—because within the next hour, her parents will be arriving. They always leave their apartment before the sun has stretched and yawned in preparation for another day. They always stop every ninety minutes to fill their stomachs with coffee and food and the car with gas. And they always arrive around 1:30 pm to give them time to unload and settle in before Peter and Sarah return from school.

It is now high noon and Vera, like Gary Cooper, must either act or leave town. She has been Peter's mother for sixteen years and Sarah's mother for fourteen years, but she has been under Ma's spell for over four decades. She once had her children's love ("When we grow up, Mommy, we're gonna each build a house on either side of yours and live there forever and ever!"). Hopefully, she will one day regain that love from them.

Ma's love, however, has been a different story. It has always hovered like the ring on a carousel that looms just beyond the rider's reach. Without one more second wasted on reflection, morality, or consequences, Vera makes her decision: Ma over kids.

She opts to begin with Peter's room since it contains less rage than Sarah's. The door to Peter's room is hard to open because, as Vera realizes once she has huffed and puffed and almost blown it down, Peter has created a barrier with his dirty clothes. Books cover the bed, while the bookshelves Vera had painstakingly put together stand empty. The only part of Peter's room that radiates with cleanliness is the area that contains his stereo and keyboard.

Although Vera has not been in Sarah's room since her daughter has made at least two furniture changes, Vera knows Ma will head directly to it. "It's one thing to let a son live in squalor, but you cannot allow your daughter—a lady—to live in such a mess!"

What amazes Vera is that Ma can snap these words at her without ever seeming to move her lips from their straight line of disdain.

Ma had never thought of Vera's room as off-bounds to her. The issue of privacy became a non-issue in a house that Ma ran and in the life of a daughter that Ma controlled. Ma used to enter Vera's room first thing in the morning, turning on the overhead light even before Vera's alarm awakened her for the day. As Vera would stretch and make the transition from night to day, Ma would be holding the bedspread in anticipation of flinging it across the bed.

By the time Vera returned from performing her daily ablutions in the bathroom, Ma had not only made the bed but had also dusted the dresser (re-arranging Vera's cologne bottles and picture frames), re-organized the papers on the desk (inadvertently hiding the science paper due that day under notebooks from English and social studies), and not-so-subtly hinted at what Vera should wear by arranging clothes on the bed so they looked like Vera's favorite childhood doll that her older brother had dismembered and beheaded.

Peter sulks when Vera messes with his room, but Sarah reacts with a psychotic fury. Should Vera dare to throw anything away—even something as benign as a dirty tissue—Sarah spends the next hours and days emoting about why she is fated to live in such bondage where nothing—not even a dried-up apple (that really does look like Ma Bates's skeletal head)—is immune from Vera's intrusion. Even when Vera tries to surreptitiously dust under a pencil holder or pick up a bent paper clip from the floor, Sarah knows—and she never lets Vera forget.

Clothes, like the shriveled, brittle leaves of winter, litter the beige carpet stained by drops of soda dribbling from overturned cans. The bedspread, the blue printed one Sarah loves so much, lays half on the bed and half on the floor. It turns the room into a distorted Smurf-colored village of bridges made from books, mountains built out of magazines, and plateaus created by paper. Metal hangars, weighed down by too many articles of clothing, fight each other for space in the closet that reeks like week-old cheese. Vera is convinced that she sees something crawl from the closet to the safety of an under-the-bed-spot, but she decides not to pursue that image. Instead, she just stands there, mindlessly rubbing the pimple that seems to have grown larger in this unsanitary environment.

Vera fights the impulse to leave the room in its inglorious messiness, but she cannot ignore the nagging voice reminding her that Ma equates the messy room of the child (particularly the daughter) with the poor parenting skills of the mother. Taking a deep breath that momentarily loosens the pressure from the elastic waistband of her sweatpants, Vera turns off her mind as if it has been anesthetized and, like a robot, re-hangs clothes, arranges shoes by matching pairs, sprays and dusts, clears and stacks. While Vera does throw out the brown lunch bag with the rock-hard bagel lying under a brown loafer, she does not turn every imperfection into perfection. Like a tightrope walker who stumbles and bumbles without a net, Vera dupes herself into believing that she has cleaned just enough for Sarah not to notice but for Ma to be satisfied.

With little time to spare, Vera changes into a less garish blue pants suit and then perches atop the bathroom sink so she can closely examine her nose. She spends the next ten minutes applying hot compresses to the mountainous mound, but instead of bringing the pimple to a head, she only succeeds in enflaming it. Just as she begins to paint her nose with foundation, the doorbell rings.

Once again, Vera trudges down the steps. She almost hopes she will fall like she did the year before because Ma will certainly care more about a concussion and broken right foot than a bulbous nose and messy bedrooms. Vera, however, reaches the foyer without a mishap. She opens the door and melts at Dad's warm grin, welcoming kiss on the head, and hug that eradicates images of Peter's sullen eyes, Sarah's angry glare, and Ma's disapproving scowl. Feeling fortified, Vera looks over Dad's shoulder and sees the packages and boxes of food crammed into the back seat of the car.

"Where's Ma?" Vera asks.

Dad, who usually looks directly at Vera, whether or not her nose has doubled in size, now seems to be studying something just above and beyond Vera's head.

"Where's Ma?" Vera repeats.

"You remember Mary, the owner of the boutique where Ma works, don't you? Well, Mary's sister got sick so she asked Ma if she could watch the store this weekend so she could be with her.

And Ma agreed." Dad speaks in a rush, as if he will choke if he keeps the words inside for even one more second.

"Ma didn't come so she could manage the boutique for Mary?" Even as Vera foolishly repeats the words, hoping that she misheard Dad, she knows that Ma has once again pledged her allegiance to her job, not to her family. The dress boutique job that began thirty years ago as part-time now consumes Ma.

Before her death, Grandma had said it best: "Your mother, Vera, has sold her soul to the company store."

"C'mon, Vera, help me unload the car. Ma has spent weeks cooking and packing dinners for you and the kids."

Dad gives Vera another kiss on the head and then returns to the car. Vera just stands in her dust-free foyer leading into her perfectly polished first floor, descending to her spider-free basement, and ascending into her sparkling second floor. She wonders if she has enough time to re-enter her children's bedrooms and restore messiness to the order she has created. The roaring of the engine as Peter soars into the parking space next to Dad's car tells her it is too late.

Vera watches in silence as Peter and Sarah rush to Grandpa and hug and kiss him. She hears them ask about Grandma and spend a minute mourning her absence before racing towards their rooms. She hears their separate gasps, followed by their voices melding into one primal shout of anger and betrayal: "Shit, Ma, what have you done? Why have you messed with my room?"

Vera does not respond to the wrath exploding from her children and to the intense sorrow emanating from Dad. Instead, she feverishly scratches the bleeding lump on her nose, hoping to lose herself in the physical pain of the infection. But nothing can stop her from imagining Ma, the queen of push 'n shove, standing in Mary's boutique and happily selling a silk scarf or cashmere sweater, oblivious to the chaos she has created in the already fragile life of her daughter.

Nothing can stop Vera from knowing that she has again lost the possibility of maybe hearing Ma exclaim, "Wow, Vera, the house looks great, and you look great. After all, pimples are a sign of character!" Vera mourns for Dad, for her children, and for herself, the adult child who misses the mother she never had.

Rubbing her bloodied fingers on her blue pants, Vera trudges to her kitchen to defrost a meal that no one has the appetite to eat.

About the author:

As a part-time faculty member of the University of Pittsburgh's English Department, Ronna works as a consultant at the school's Writing Center. She also teaches Freshman Programs, a course that introduces students to the University and the city. Her work, both fiction and nonfiction, has appeared in *Quality Women's Fiction*; *Ghoti Online Literary Magazine*; *First Line Anthology*; *The Road to Elsewhere* (Scribes Valley Publishing); *Welcome to Elsewhere* (Scribes Valley Publishing); *SLAB: Sound and Literary Artbook*; *Pulse: Voices from the Heart of Medicine* (online magazine); AARP Bulletin (online); *Healthy Roots* (Forbes Health Foundation and Hospice); and the *Pittsburgh Post-Gazette*.

THE COMMITMENT
©2011 by Pat Decker Nipper

As soon as I read about George Holly's death, I felt a profound sorrow. His wife had been like part of my family when I was growing up and I was acquainted with him mainly through phone calls, where he'd always joke with me. I was fond of them both.

I called Mrs. Holly to give her my condolences but she didn't answer her phone until the eighth ring. I knew she had become hard of hearing so I waited. When she finally answered, I identified myself.

Twice.

"Hello, Mrs. Holly. This is Amy Mix. You used to babysit for me. Do you remember?"

"Who?"

"Amy Mix. You used to be my nanny."

"Little Amy? Of course. But I don't do any sitting these days. I'm retired."

"I know. I'm not calling about that. I wanted to say how sorry I was to hear of George's death," I said.

"It was so sudden, you know," she said. "One minute he was fine. The next minute he just keeled over. Massive coronary the doctor said. I miss him every day."

"It's truly sad. He was very nice to me. Is there anything I can do for you? Maybe you'd like to come for dinner. I would love to cook for you."

"How sweet! I can't do anything now, though. I have taxes,

53

insurance..."

"That's all right. Shall I call you then next month?"

"That would be lovely. I'll have a month to catch up on everything. Thank you for remembering George."

And with that, she hung up. What? No good-bye? Well, she was getting up in years and she had a lot on her mind.

I let six weeks go by, knowing I should phone her. She could be waiting for my call. On the other hand, I was pretty busy. It would be hard to squeeze in time for a dinner, especially one I had to cook.

Finally, my conscience made me phone Mrs. Holly again. A commitment must be honored. Her phone rang and rang until the answer phone kicked in. It was one of those impersonal messages where you never know if you have dialed the right number. "There is no one home. Please leave a message." So, I left a message and hung up.

I called later that evening and got the same message. This, I thought, was odd. I knew Mrs. Holly didn't go out much after dark. Maybe her habits were changing now that she was a widow. I waited until after ten, then tried again. Still the same message. Something could be wrong with her phone, or maybe she had started to do some babysitting again.

The next day I tried again, got no results, checked with 4-1-1 to be sure I had the right number, then, because I was busy, decided to give it another day. Finally, on the third day, a Saturday, with still no answer on the phone, I drove to the Holly home. There was no car in the driveway. I rang the doorbell, but all I heard was a barking dog. In fact, the dog sounded frantic.

Oh-oh. Something must be wrong.

I walked over to the neighbor's house and knocked on the door. A woman answered.

"Hi, I'm Amy Mix," I said. "I'm trying to get hold of Mrs. Holly. She doesn't seem to be home. Do you know where she's gone?"

"Oh, hello. I'm Emily Groves. I believe Mrs. Holly left a couple of days ago. At least that's when she drove off in her car."

"Her dog is in the house and seems very upset."

"I know, he's been barking and barking. It isn't like her to leave him shut up like that."

"Do you think she's all right?"

"Hmm. I wonder. I haven't seen anybody over there and that dog, Skipper, thinks he's starving."

"Maybe he is," I said. "I think we should find a way in and feed the dog."

Poor Skipper was whining and scratching on the windows, following us as we moved around the house.

"I agree, but both doors are locked. I already tried them. For the dog, you know."

"How about a window?" We circled the house again, finally finding a bathroom window cracked open. Unfortunately, it was about fifteen feet above ground. "Guess most people wouldn't try to get in that window," I said.

"I have a ladder," Emily said. "It should be long enough, but you'll have to help carry it. It's quite heavy."

We marched over to her house, found the ladder in the garage, and hauled it over to Mrs. Holly's bathroom window. I volunteered to climb up and crawl in the window. Emily was happy to let me be the one to risk my neck.

I started up the rungs. The wooden ladder was old and not in the best condition. When I heard the first rung crack, I avoided it and went on up. Carefully. When I reached the top of the ladder, I was just below the window. I struggled to unhook the screen and raise the window far enough to get inside. I had to let go of the ladder and boost myself up and in. When I was halfway in, I realized the toilet was directly below and the seat was up.

Dang.

Then Skipper discovered me and started barking. Maybe he'd been getting his drinks from the toilet. This probably kept him alive, since it might have been several days since he'd had any attention.

"That's okay, Skipper," I said. "I'm here to give you your

dinner!" At that, he began to wag his tail. "Dinner" was apparently a word he understood.

I tried to lower the toilet seat, but the motion tipped me beyond my balance point and I began to fall.

"No-o-o," I moaned as my left arm hit the toilet bowl. I felt a tremendous pain as the rest of me followed. I didn't hit the water, which was a blessing, and I was clearly inside the house, but pains were shooting up my arm.

"What's happening?" Emily called.

"I'm in," I shouted, "but I've hurt my arm. It might be broken."

"Oh, dear. Shall I call an ambulance?"

"No need. I'll open the front door and you can help me feed the dog. Then maybe you can drive me to the emergency room."

"Of course."

After we got the dog fed we drove to the clinic. I wondered what had happened to Mrs. Holly. Was she all right?

Emily was thinking the same thing. "I don't think Mrs. Holly went shopping. Tuesday was her shopping day, four days ago."

"Do you think she went to the cemetery where her husband is buried?"

"It's possible, but he was buried in Spring Wood."

"How far is that? Fifty miles?"

"Probably closer to eighty. He was born there."

"Is she able to drive that far?"

Emily laughed. "Well, she *shouldn't* drive that far, that's for sure. Her eyes aren't very good and she's forgetful. Her son drove her to the funeral."

"Maybe we should call her son. Do you have his number?"

"No, but we can probably find his number in the Holly's house."

After I got a cast on my arm, we drove back to the Holly's and found a phone number for their son Tom.

He was no help. "I don't know where she is, but I'll come over and get the dog, bring him home with me. She's probably visiting some old friends. Let me know when you find her," he said, and rang off.

Emily helped me call her friends. A number of them must have either died or moved but she hadn't crossed off their phone numbers. Others who were home and able to answer the phone didn't know where she could be. There weren't many friends left.

"Maybe she took a trip," a woman named Mathilda said. "She was always talking about wanting to travel, but George wouldn't hear of it."

"Would she take her car?" I asked. "It's gone."

"Well, no, she'd probably take a taxi if she was flying or taking the train. Well, if you find her, tell her to call. It's been ages since we've had a chance to chat."

Emily said, "Let's drive around and try to find her car. She has an older model Chevy sedan, blue. If we don't see it, we'll call the police and tell them she's missing."

"Good idea—as long as you drive."

We decided to go to Spring Wood first, on the assumption that Mrs. Holly might be visiting Mr. Holly's grave. The town was in a rural and rather mountainous area and we soon found ourselves on a two-lane road. While we passed farms and forests, I enjoyed the scenery, though my arm throbbed—even with the pain pills from the hospital.

I also scoured the roadside, but I saw no blue car. "Maybe she didn't come this way after all."

"If we don't find her, we'll go back and check the parking lots close to home."

When we arrived in Spring Wood, we drove straight to the cemetery, which could have been larger than the town, which seemed to have its future behind it. However, there were no cars parked in the lot. We checked the lots near churches, motels, and shopping areas, before finally deciding this search was useless.

"Let's get lunch before we go back," Emily said.

It was already after two. "Good idea. The cherry pie at the Knot Hole cafe in Spring Wood is legendary."

We had the pie for dessert and it lived up to its reputation. On the way home, we resumed our search. By now it was getting close to sunset. Suddenly I saw something that made me sit up straight. "Wait!" I shouted. "I think I see skid marks. There might have been an accident."

She pulled over and we got out of the car. The skid marks left the roadway and the shoulder and went over the edge, which was quite steep. Of course, we had no way of knowing if these marks were recent, but as we looked, we could see the weeds crushed, bushes disturbed. We couldn't see farther than the brow of the hill.

"If there's a car down there now," Emily said, "it's out of sight."

"I saw a reflection off something metal. I'll go down and look."

"It's very steep. You only have one arm. How can you manage? Maybe we should call somebody."

"It could be an old junker. I should check." I thought for a moment. "Do you have a rope in the car?"

Emily went back and raised the trunk. "Yes, there's one in here. My husband must have left it there before he deployed. Looks like a long one, too."

"Good. I'll tie it around my waist and we can anchor it to the car, then you can lower me down the hill."

"Okay. Hope I'm strong enough."

I hoped so, too, as I tied the rope round my waist. Emily got down and tied the other end around the axel. She did such a good job of that, I was growing more confident that she could lower me all right.

"I'll play out the rope as you go down," she said. "If it looks too difficult, come back up. We'll call for help."

I began inching down the hill, holding the rope tightly with my right hand. The bushes were dense and scratchy and I used my left arm to push them aside. The cast protected me somewhat. I hoped there was no poison oak growing in there.

I didn't have to go very far before I could see a car with a person's head leaning against the window. Whether it was Mrs. Holly or not, I hoped she was just asleep. "Okay, Emily, haul me up. We need to call for a tow truck. And an ambulance."

"Did you see Mrs. Holly?"

"I saw a blue car and there was a head resting against the driver's side window."

"Was she alive? Could you tell?"

"I couldn't tell. She might be unconscious or asleep."

Emily had pulled me up by now and was rubbing her arms. "I need to go back to the gym and get in shape," she muttered as she found her cell phone.

After some twenty minutes, the rural fire department arrived, followed closely by an ambulance and the state police. We watched as an agile fireman made his way down the hillside—without a rope. He attached the tow truck's hook to the car, scrambled back up, and signaled the driver to start winching the car up.

As soon as the car was back on the road, the fire department went to work on the crushed car door, using the Jaws of Life. When they got it open, they carefully extracted Mrs. Holly.

"She's alive!" the EMT shouted, "but she's out cold."

"Do you think she'll be all right?" I asked as they put her in the ambulance.

"Hard to say," he told me. "She's probably injured and dehydrated. We'll have to wait and see."

Emily and I followed the ambulance to the closest hospital, which happened to be in Spring Wood, and got Mrs. Holly checked in to the emergency ward. We called her son and told him what had happened.

"Bring your mother's Medicare card," I added.

After he arrived, he joined us in the waiting room. One of the nurses said that Mrs. Holly had suffered several injuries and the doctors were giving her a lot of tests and patching her up."

Finally, after she was moved to a regular room, we were allowed to visit her, one at a time. When it was my turn, I stood by her bed and asked how she was feeling. "Hi, Mrs. Holly. It's Amy Mix, all grown up. How do you feel?"

"Not so good," she said, taking my hand. "I hurt all over. I see you have a cast, too. How did you hurt yourself?"

"It's a long story. Suffice it to say we both had quite an

adventure. It started when I tried to find you and follow up on my commitment."

She stared at me, my arm in a cast, my face scratched by bushes. "Commitment? What commitment?"

"Remember? I called you to say I was sorry about George's death and asked if you'd like to come to dinner. You said to wait a month, so I did. When I called, you weren't home, so then I tried to find you. Your neighbor and I went looking until we saw your car down that ravine."

She stared harder. None of this seemed to be making much sense to her. Finally, she said, "Well, thank you, dear. I appreciate it. Now, what was that commitment again?"

I don't know how I thought Mrs. Holly would react, but I hadn't expected her to forget the entire invitation. All that I went through, thinking I'd made a commitment—I could have just skipped the whole thing. She had not been waiting for my phone call at all. I would not have disappointed her if I'd never followed up.

Oh, well, the old girl wouldn't be here today if I hadn't bothered.

About the author:

Pat Decker Nipper is a native of Idaho, now living and writing in San Jose, California. She has written several short stories, including "The Idaho Gold Dust Murders," published in James Crutchfield's anthology *The Way West: True Stories of the American Frontier*, and "Who Really Killed President Lincoln?" appearing in the collection of short stories: *Black Hats*, by Robert Randisi. Her book *Love on the Lewis and Clark Trail* was published in 2004. She has had a number of articles printed, including three in Wild West magazine, and one in True West magazine. She has written a brief grammar column, "Nipper's Nits," which can be read on her web site, www.patdeckernipper.com.

BACHAN SEKEI, THE NAKED LADIES, AND ME
©2011 by Jean Tschohl Quinn

I'd like to apologize. The harvest of 1965 that just petered out and the drought of the following winter were my fault. Mine...and Mrs. Sekei's. I know it was a long time ago and the frustration of the rotten harvest is long forgotten, mixed in with vague memories of bumper crops, but it still bothers me. If you'd be so kind, will you listen to my confession? I think Mrs. Sekei would have approved.

I grew up in Corralitos on several acres that neighbored Mrs. Sekei's property. Our houses were situated so that we could see into each other's kitchens. She had a small stucco house with a large garden corralled by a picket fence; my folks' property extended far into the distance. Once, she mentioned that her family owned much of the area...until the War. I wasn't sure what to make of that, but I liked her, her tidy garden, and the time we spent together there.

Sometime in August of '65, we were tending the long, hot row of pole beans that bordered the fence. She straightened up, not making herself much taller than when she was stooped over. Adjusting her Japanese gardening hat, a contraption that looked remarkably similar to a straw lampshade, Bachan—that's the Japanese word for grandmother; any lady with gray hair was referred to as Grandma: *Avó* for the Portuguese ones, *Abuelita* for the Mexicanas—squinted into the distance. "Dagnabbit. They've come already."

I stopped to peer in the same direction, but saw only the parched, golden fallow fields alternating with endless rows of green irrigated lettuce and artichoke of the flat Pajaro Valley. "Who's come, Bachan?"

She wiped her upper lip with a kerchief from her apron pocket, "It's those naked ladies."

As cute as the naked ladies standing on the side of the road are, Bachan disliked seeing them. Their faces were invariably bright and sunburn pink; their stems long, smooth, brown and completely bare. Each leg supported at least four of the perky trumpets. *Lycoris squamigera*, my high school biology teacher would tell me a few years later, is a type of amaryllis imported from Japan since the 1880s.

Why did she harbor such ill will to the cheery, cheeky lilies? I asked her.

"Because they are harbingers of autumn. They poke their flashy heads up, showing off with no green to support them. Then they shrivel up and remind me of my own shriveled up body." She spat. "I lost too much of my youth to this valley and don't like to be reminded of it." She shuffled off toward the back porch of her house, mumbling, "But this year, I'm ready for 'em."

I chased after her with a basket of beans in each hand, both her basket and mine.

She kept mumbling, "Once they die off, the nights get cold and my old bones ache. Once that starts, the rains follow soon enough. No, these old bones don't like the rain one bit."

I concentrated on preparing the green beans for canning. With an old Swiss army knife that she used for just about everything, she trimmed and chopped four beans to every one of mine.

When putting away the baskets and gardening tools in the shed, I noticed stacks of large boxes in and behind it. They hadn't been there the week before. She was clearly in no mood for questions, so I ran home for supper with the mystery unsolved.

That night when the hall clock struck midnight, an engine

coughed. I peered out my window just in time to see her drive off into the darkness with two of the mysterious boxes in the back of her '38 Chevy truck. The next morning, the truck was back, its bed empty. The next night, it was the same. On the third night, I sneaked out of the house as soon as everyone else was asleep, ran to the truck, hopped in the back and hid myself under a filthy tarp that lived there. I waited quietly amid the dust and desiccated mildew as she emerged from the house, unknowingly placed two boxes next to me, and drove off.

I peeked out as we—the boxes and I—bounced along the road. Once the engine coughed to a stop, I pulled the tarp back over my head. The tailgate creaked downwards. Then I sneezed. Mrs. Sekei snatched the tarp quickly. Her narrowed eyes flickered alarm, then recognition. She put her fingers to her lips. We were just outside the entrance to Mann's Apple Farm.

She shrugged and commenced a perplexing, whispered explanation: "You call him Jack Frost, but in Japan, it is *Susanowo*." She paused and frowned, "That's all I remember about him. In any case, he brings on autumn." With a raise of her chin, she signaled me to push a box towards her. I did. Three deft swipes with her trusty knife and a box sprang open. "Jack Frost is near-sighted," she hissed in the night, "and most other folks are just plain blind."

I skootched on my rump to the tailgate to get a peek at the contents. The moonlight shone, flashing pink, bright pink. She reached into the box and pulled out the contents, almost reverently. She raised the contents aloft for my inspection in silence. Except for the mischievous glint in her black eyes, she registered no indication that I was in utter confusion. Silhouetted against the moonlight-drenched orchard, her tiny frame stood there with two pink flamingoes in each hand as high as her arthritic shoulders could muster, shaking them at some distant, cold wind.

I sputtered. She lowered her arms disappointedly, setting her fists akimbo on her hips, flanked by the plastic birds. Her beetle eyes betrayed her dis-appointment in my lack of understanding, "We're hiding them amongst the naked ladies to fool Jack Frost. If he doesn't think it's time, he won't bring on autumn."

Thus, that is what we did every night until dozens of boxes lay flattened and empty in her shed. For fourteen days, I climbed out my window at midnight and ran across the field to load the truck. She had plotted precisely where to plant the lawn ornaments for the first week. I made suggestions from notes I took on a Sunday trip to my grandparents. The last three nights, we surreptitiously scanned the countryside around Aromas with flashlights.

On the first day of school, I jumped on the bus expecting to hear hubbub about the pink flamingos popping up all over the countryside, but there was nothing. Naked ladies dotted the roadsides, fields, and gardens mixed in with their new avian friends. Still no one noticed. The weeks passed and the lilies faded and shriveled up. Eventually, they lay down to rest on the sere, dusty ground. Still no one noticed. September melted into October. October ran into November with only passing comments about the weather being strange for the time of year. December, January, and February faded into one another. The apples never quite ripened. The winter crops didn't even bother to sprout.

Sometime around Saint Valentine's Day, I pleaded meekly, "I think we have to undo our trickery."

"But my limbs don't ache. And my roses are still blooming."

"Mrs. Sekei," I scolded.

She scoffed, "I knew you didn't really understand."

"Bachan," I pleaded, "we stopped one harvest. We can't stop spring from coming too!"

She sighed a heavy, burdened sigh, "You're right. You could start tonight, I guess."

"*We will* start tonight." I crossed my arms for emphasis. She spat in response, but I held my ground.

That very night, we collected hundreds of pink flamingoes. For five nights straight, we rumbled about the countryside and little towns of Santa Cruz, San Benito, and Monterey Counties. By day, I fell asleep on the bus, dozed at my desk, and collapsed at the dinner table. By night, we prowled. We had collected them all—all but a few near her house.

She winked at me, "I just want to remind old Jack Frost just who fooled him."

In time, the Seasons corrected themselves and the rhythms returned. I grew up and Mrs. Sekei passed away. And, I guess, Jack Frost is still near-sighted.

About the author:

This story will be Jean's fourth appearance in a Scribes Valley anthology. One of her stories also appears in *Under the Rose* by Norilana Press. She has helped to edit a local anthology. As their three daughters fly from their nest amongst the redwoods and fruit trees along the Central Coast of Cailifornia, she and her husband have unwittingly begun a collection of certified preowned antique dogs. She really needs to get a job, although she cannot imagine going back to mathematics.

Ya Baha'ul'Abha!

ANNOUNCEMENT
©2011 by Steve Breitzka

I expected dank. A rich, moist smell that clung to the walls. I wanted this to be a memorable day. I was not disappointed after snaking through the empty security line and being told to remove my belt by a man who had clearly added a few holes to his. The sun had been shining in the parking lot, but there was a cold, manufactured light inside. The guard grunted or burped or woke up and motioned for me to move forward. There were no lights blinking on the metal detector. No fancy "green means go" or "red means assume the position" indicators. There was no sign that the detector was even on. It had a slight tilt to it like it had been made out of recycled lumber and slapped with a new coat of clearance-rack beige paint.

My belt was waiting for me in the inspective hands of the grumpy guard's accomplice. "This your belt?" she asked, looking at my chest, disinterested in me but clearly fascinated with my belt.

I looked around, just the three of us. I wondered whose belt she thought it could be. Was she trying to make polite conversation and this was the one thing we had in common? My belt? Her fingers seemed to be enjoying the experience too much.

"Yes, ma'am," I responded, not used to calling people ma'am and sir, but these people were pretty close to law enforcement.

"Nice belt. I like it," she said, running her fingertips over the leather.

The only thing I was sure of at this point was my level of

discomfort. Was I supposed to thank her? Did she have a belt fetish? If she smelled it, I swore I was going to turn around and run away, gladly paying whatever fine necessary.

"Umm, thank you," I responded with my hand out.

"You're free to go," she said, laying my belt down on the table.

I wasn't completely certain she was talking to me.

There was a sad yellow arrow pointing down the only available hallway. I moved along despite any actual direction that I was supposed to follow that particular arrow. A persistent, low hum vibrated off the walls, like there was some massive machine behind one of the doors. The kind of droning sound that gets trapped in your head.

The hall ended with two glass doors covered with an uneven film. *Or is that steam?* I thought, standing there with my hands frozen at my sides, the vibration making my muscles tense. *What is on the other side of these doors?*

I wanted there to be a rotund man on the other side, wearing thick glasses and a wrinkled white shirt with a pocket protector and one glaring coffee stain. He would jabber as though every word running out of his mouth was the most important word you should hear. Questions would be met with a sigh, a quick breath, and faster repetition. His sniffling assistant would scribble on a notepad too small for notes and squint at nothing in particular.

The door handle glistened. Was it polished? Was it wet? I leaned in for a closer look when the door opened. Part of me wanted to look down and see an orange Oompa-Loompa looking up at me, beckoning me into the funhouse. Instead I saw a blur of a man, apparently in search of a bathroom, rush past me.

I stepped into the room and noticed that I couldn't distinguish the back wall to the left or the right. Was this some sort of clever painting? I wondered. The walls were a pale, cheap shade of green frozen by the florescent bars above. This was the interior designer equivalent of a stomach ache.

I approached the front desk, not really sure if I was supposed to check in or sit.

"Card," the woman behind the desk said.

"I'm sorry?" I asked her, instantly feeling her resentment toward me.

"Your card!" she belted, reaching out her hand.

"Umm...I...what?" I asked, leaning over the desk, like having her repeat her brief rant would help.

"I can't check you in without a complete, signed card," she said, glaring at me. She had stressed the word *you* and darted her head like I had been here yesterday and I had made the same mistake.

I looked at the yellow card she held. Had this been created on a typewriter? The questions it asked had a uniform yet uneven quality, like they all carried the same important weight but they had been created with a fierce frustration. I stared at the black, punched font. Name, address, sex, and the usual demographic suspects.

The clerk's oppressive squint pulled me down. Was I slowing the process? Was everyone else in line up to speed on this process? How could I be "that guy?" I accepted the rectangle she presented to me. There was a box of unsharpened golf pencils on the desk next to her stained coffee mug. A dark maroon print marked the edge of her cup although she did not appear to be wearing lipstick.

I selected a pencil with a dull slant of graphite and began scratching in my name. "Do you have a pencil sharpener?" I asked, assuming the answer. Others in the delinquent line looked up, hopeful.

"No," she coughed.

I looked back at the card and then I decided to press my luck, "I'm sorry but why do you need my name and address?"

"Because we need you to fill out the card and the card needs your name and address."

"But," I was attempting to choose my words carefully before she lashed out and bit me, "you mailed me the summons."

She stared.

I stared.

The other pencil holders put their heads down and continued.

My eyes eventually rolled left, right, and officially broke her stare. I focused and etched in my name. Her eyes stayed on me until I finished and handed the card to her.

"Thank you for your cooperation," she sneered.

My mouth draped. A fly twitched its thin legs against her ear. The cool blue lights illuminated the fine bristles of ear hair that were being tickled by the fly's lightest touches. The fly tip-toed slowly, inspecting as it moved. I could hear it in my own ears: that weak buzz. I watched it step delicately over the rim of her ear and then stop, as though peering into a cavern.

Please brush that away! I screamed in my mind. She did not. She sat there. The fly continued and hung from her lobe like a fidgety earring. We all stared. I automatically reached up and rubbed both of my ears. Was it on me now?

The clerk went about her business, collecting our cards. She issued a terse hiss and asked each one of us to fill them out in advance next time. Apparently, a note had been typed along the bottom edge instructing attendees to arrive with completed cards. None of us saw it.

Knowing that whatever I said would be met with some sort of waiting room punishment, I stepped away and faced my summoned colleagues for the first time. The word "peer" did not come to mind. I spotted an empty section of seats toward the back and decided I would have a good vantage point of whatever was about to happen.

There was a man sleeping in the front row. He looked like an upright puddle that had dripped into the chair. His camouflaged t-shirt gave a slight rise and at least some reassurance that he was still breathing. My foot stuck to the carpet. I looked down and saw a wet patch. *Was that dripping from above?* I asked myself. A woman behind me cleared her throat indicating I was in her way.

"Sorry," I said, looking down at her and then up at the brown stain that was engulfing the ceiling. A golden drip formed in the center and dropped. I turned to walk to the open seats and found a short, balding man wearing a blue and white horizontal-striped shirt and green shorts standing before me.

"Smoke," he said, shaking his hand.

"I'm sorry?" I asked, not sure if he was asking or offering.

"Do you smoke?" he coughed at me.

"Sorry, no." I replied.

He grunted and moved on.

I took a chair surrounded by empty seats and absorbed the room. Was my chair vibrating? I could feel the same hum I heard earlier. I watched people file in through the main door, each one judging their new surroundings. Some walked right in like they did this every day. Others, a surprising and disturbing minority, crossed the threshold and looked like they had just smelled a rotten potato.

We were supposed to be checked in and seated by 8:30. The clock above the clerk read 9:35. Did they set it five minutes fast one day and then forget to fall back in October, or were they just messing with us?

My watch read 8:30 on the nose, and I was on the edge of my seat for the first announcement. The faded brown cloth speaker on the wall next to me was emitting a constant crackle. It suddenly popped, like someone had flicked the microphone.

Please stand by for an important announcement, came through the static with a vacant voice.

I sat up straight. How did this work? Who would be selected? How elaborate could this possibly be?

Five minutes passed. Six. Seven. My shoulders slumped. Apparently, the announcement was not that important after all.

I heard a toilet flush. *Where in the hell did that come from?* I asked myself.

Part of me expected the dripping ceiling tile to come crashing down with a gush of whatever had just been flushed. A door opened to my left and a man stepped out with a newspaper under one arm and a very satisfied look on his face. He looked like a Roy. Maybe Leroy, but that sounded geeky and he gave up being a geek in the eighth grade when he realized girls were more fun than

Dungeons and Dragons. So now he goes by Roy.

Was that a bathroom? Why wasn't the door marked? Is that why these seats were all empty? How did everyone know that but me? I was trying to decide if I should move when the smell pushed me to a new seat. I expected to turn and see a cartoon cloud of stink moving toward me. There were open seats all over the place, but each one seemed to be the separating open space between two people. I would instantly become the third wheel between two strangers. Maybe I would meet someone intriguing and our conversation would blur the time until the day was just over.

Deciding to take a chance, I spotted a chair toward the front between two women; one who looked like she had stopped here on her way to a biker rally and the other who looked like June Cleaver. I figured if they could tolerate each other, a little company wouldn't hurt.

I walked slowly up the aisle, choosing my path wisely to avoid the wet spots in the carpet. The whole room, other than the clock, moved slowly. Why didn't anyone else notice this? The light above me went out. It flickered once, and then nothing. I focused on the biker and June and pushed through.

The biker stared at her magazine. How did she snap her gum that loud? It sounded like she was chewing on a firecracker. She did not move to let me pass by. I said, "Excuse me," but I don't think she heard me, saw me, or cared. I imagined she had a tough sounding biker-chick kind of name like Jo or Bert—short for Alberta—but no one knew that about her, and no one questions a girl named Bert. Or maybe she went by a nickname like Skidz or Spokes or some other motorcycle term.

The chair squeaked when I sat down. A plastic chair with metal legs on a carpet floor. I tried to determine what squeaked. June turned and offered a perfunctory smile. I had never seen someone sit that upright. I straightened my back, pushed back my shoulders and still felt like I was slouching.

I sat with my hands in my lap feeling claustrophobic. I suddenly missed my toilet seat. It was one thing to up and leave a section of empty chairs, but if I did that now, both June and Bert would likely think I didn't appreciate their silent and erect company. I couldn't have that on my conscience. Besides, the sweet flower patch smell of June's perfume, mixed with the raw tannery smell of Bert's leather ensemble, made me forget Leroy's bowel movement.

June unclasped her purse and withdrew a chocolate chip cookie.

Of course, I thought, *of course she carries cookies in her purse.* I figured they were sandwiched between wadded tissues and ketchup packets. She took a tiny bite of the cookie and put it away as though she was handling a bomb. Was she rationing it? Expecting to be here for the long haul and surviving on bad coffee and one cookie?

I hadn't brought my coffee in with me. I didn't know if that was allowed, and judging by the controversy my belt caused, I was glad I had left my mug in the car. But I smelled coffee. Or really just hot liquid. There was the sense of steam in the air. I saw a man walk around the corner holding a Styrofoam cup. He must have gotten that here, I figured. No one leaves the house with a Styrofoam cup. Do they?

"I'm going to get some coffee," burst out of my mouth. *Wait, did I just say that out loud?* I had to ask myself.

Bert continued to perfect her scowl.

"Excuse me, dear?" June sang.

"Umm...right," I said, getting up, moving away, and feeling my face burst into flame all at once. What was that? I didn't even know these people.

The speakers popped again. I stopped in my tracks like a prison searchlight had just found me.

Again, please standby for an important announcement, blurted out quickly like one long word.

My body was rigid. Either my feet were stuck to the carpet again or fear had gripped me. Was this announcement somehow about me and talking to strangers? I expected to hear, *Sit down!*

There is no coffee! come booming down upon me.

I managed to rip my feet free and move toward the corner. There was an unnatural stack of Styrofoam cups leaning against a giant silver missile of a coffeemaker. The enormous, silver canister coffee pot reminded me of church basement potlucks. I lost myself in thoughts of overcooked pasta and fruit drowned in Jell-O.

There was that little orange light that somehow communicated the coffee, or brownish liquid inside, was ready. No one else was standing here. I knew by the crowd that I shouldn't bother, but wouldn't it be great if there was some shining moment for this experience? Like, in ten years I could say to my sons, "On that day, I drank the best damn cup of coffee I've ever tasted." What a legacy to pass on.

I lifted a cup and felt that Styrofoam-on-Styrofoam friction. The rubbing made the hair on my arms stand on end. I held the cup under the spigot and lifted the lever. Nothing. Not even a teasing drip. Maybe if I tilted it? That was when I noticed the coffee pot was bolted down.

"Really?" I mumbled. Were they worried this three-foot-high, two-foot-wide silver antique of a coffee pot might get stolen? How would that even work? Someone saunters over all casual and suave-looking only to swipe the pot in one swift motion and break for the door? This thing may not even fit *through* the door. And then what would this Super-Thief do? Hide it and dash past security?

"Excuse me, sir, is that a coffee pot from 1972 under your shirt?" I could imagine the guard with the belt fetish asking.

I decided to find out what my friend the clerk could do to help. She was sitting behind the front desk looking at something. As I got closer, I realized she was actually staring, and looking at nothing. Her mouth hung open like she was in a couch potato trance.

"Excuse me?" I asked in my most polite and apologetic voice, knowing I was interrupting whatever it was she was doing.

She looked, saying nothing.

Good God! I thought, *that fly is still attached to her ear.* I raised my hand to my mouth, hoping it looked pensive and not like I was preventing myself from blurting out, "PLEASE TOUCH YOUR EAR! ANYTHING! PLEASE?" I took a breath and lowered my hand, steadying myself. "It seems the coffee is gone," I told her.

"Yes," she replied.

I waited until it became clear she was not about to elaborate. "Would it be possible to make another pot?" I asked.

"No," she said, returning to her staring.

I didn't know what to do. In two short words she had made it rather clear that she had little desire to help me or the coffee pot.

"Umm...all right," I said, backing away and fiddling with the empty cup in my hand. Now what do I do? I can't put the cup back, but I don't want to hold it all day. I hated to throw away a cup I didn't even use that my great-grandsons wouldn't even see deteriorate. Did they even sell these cups anymore?

My thoughts were interrupted by another pop, *Announcement forthcoming, please stand by.*

"Forthcoming?" I thought. Who says forthcoming? And where is this announcement? Three times now they have teased us.

This last blast of words sounded rushed so I decided to take the first chair I could find. The seat to my right was empty, but the seat to my left was anything but. I never could understand why anyone would wear a tank-top in public and this...gentleman...was no exception. Most women can pull off a tank-top. Men, on the other hand, should give them up with overalls.

The woman two seats to my right was staring at my foot. I had decided to wear comfortable summer sandals since I didn't know if I was going to be here for two minutes or two hours. I shifted my legs just to make some sort of motion to dissuade her. It did not work. She was more casual than June. *Too* casual. Like she was here for fun. She was sprawled across her chair instead of straight and pearled. I rubbed my hands together. My preconceived excitement for the day had been dashed by sticky carpet and flies.

Another loud pop broke my blank stare. This time nothing followed it. Was that just an attempt to keep us awake? The coffee was gone so what hope did we have? At this point I just wanted to find a comfortable chair free of smells. I shifted my shoulders, my back, my whole body, hoping to find some position that would work for longer than seven minutes.

Announce what? I pleaded in my head. Were we all free to go? Give us something! Anything!

Why did no one else seem aggravated by this? Were they all so happy to be off work that this was a favorable alternative? Like their jobs were worse? What the hell did they do for a living that sitting here, in orange, cracked, plastic chairs, staring at absolutely nothing was an upgrade?

I returned to staring. My eyes fixated on the clock at the front of the room. It still read 9:35.

About the author:

Steve Breitzka fell into a tree pit when he was five years old. Now he is an experimental gardener with a Bachelor of Science in Landscape Architecture from Cornell University who just happens to love writing short stories. He is also a scratch golfer with affection for good food and fine whiskey.

Steve owes this honor and any future writing success to his amazing wife (who is supportive despite her dislike of the short-story genre), his two sons (who may well be superheroes), his family (who is always there), his 4th grade teacher Mrs. Tomashek (who gave him a green folder, in which Steve defined "short story" as an eight-page, heroic journey to the center of the earth), and Opa (who pulled him out of the tree pit).

DISCOVERY FLIGHT
©2011 by Regina Parker

The sun peaks over the horizon and stirs the sleeping sky. An array of long violet rays of light dyes the clouds pink. The neighborhood is silent except for the chirping of the birds that woke up early to get a head start. I am soothed by the rhythm of my sneakers pounding the cool pavement, damp with dew. My ponytail whips behind in the crisp morning air. Running along, I admire the conifers sprinkling the neighborhood and enriching the place with color. The evergreens are far less abundant than the naked deciduous trees, but the continual vitality of their unwavering green is a stark contrast to the ebb and flow of life in the deciduous trees. The fading sycamores, buckeyes, and birches don't hold a candle to their beauty on this cold February morning.

I make my way home and am greeted by the scent of freshly brewed coffee permeating the whole house. Lex and Eli lounge on the couch, their eyes glued to *The Fairly Odd Parents*. Mom and Dad work diligently in their office finishing up the last of a study. Three empty coffee mugs, a bowl of moldering Captain Crunch, and an open package of Chips Ahoy cookies sit atop boxes of microscope slides and scientific journals.

I toss my sweaty shirt in the hamper, neatly make my bed, and pull a sweater out of my closet. My backpack is already packed and waiting for me by the front door, and my brown paper bag lunch is sitting in the fridge. In five minutes time I clean up and hastily comb out my hair. "Have fun at school today, guys," I say as I rustle Eli's hair before taking a quick glance in the mirror and heading out the door.

It takes fifteen minutes flat to hike up Chesley Lane to East Chapel Hill High School. I file into the horrid place with two thousand other teenagers, dreading another painful day.

"Wait up, Cathy!" Juliana runs to catch up with me. "I need your bio homework before fifth period."

I purse my lips. "I'll be in Room 234 during lunch. Copy it then."

Welcome to public education. I swear I can't go two minutes in this dismal school without being bombarded for answers to homework. Do I look like a walking homework dispenser to you? It's like I have a flashing signal on my forehead that says, *Cheat off me!*

My Ironman watch beeps; class is about to begin. The hallways roar with restless teenagers. I push my way past a jock, a gaggle of trashy girls, and an assortment of Goth gang members. "Morning, Mr. Lucus," I acknowledge the security officer who wearily polices the mob of rabid animals. I catch his quick head nod before ducking into Room 12, English class.

Ms. Pernell calls role. "Ishmael Harazu," she lazily intones from behind her desk.

"Humph" A grunt from the back of the room.

"Jesus Perez."

Silence.

"Naomi Potiglini."

Silence.

"Catherine Starkey."

"Present." My clear voice ignites the dead air and bounces off the stark walls and empty desks. I hear snickering and bazooka gum popping in the back of the room.

They mock me, "Pre-a-sent", then more giggling and a high-five. A wad of chewed-up paper lands in my lap.

"Six more classes to go," I mutter to myself.

***

"Therefore, the sum of the exponents in this log function is..."

Brrinnnggg! The dismissal bell sounds and the school erupts. Ms. Dallen comes to a screeching halt in her lesson, and a stampede of kids shove out of the trailer that suffices as our classroom. I'm left hanging, as usual, waiting to hear the summation of the logarithmic equation. Each page of my notes stops dead in the middle of a topic, indicating when the bell rang.

Ms. Dallen flicks off the light as she trots out the door. I quickly jot down the homework assignment scribbled on the gray whiteboard and am the last one to leave the classroom.

I trek home from school like a pack mule, loaded down with a solid fifty pounds of textbooks. How come nobody else seems to have any books? Half the kids don't even carry a pencil! I guess girls can't balance a backpack while strutting the halls in four-inch stilettos, and the gangsters have a hard time holding their pants up with a book in hand.

Ahead, a posse of giggling girls relaxes on a pair of picnic tables. "And then, like, he said, and so I was like, yeah, and then he said..." they chatter as they simultaneously experiment with hairstyles and text messages to each other.

"Hey, Genevieve," I smile politely and wave to my middle school pal.

She ignores my hello, but I know she heard it. Genevieve hasn't spoken to me since we entered high school. The summer after eighth grade, she transformed into a cookie-cutter "flirt face" and cast me aside like a used tissue. I swallow my disappointment and continue home, followed by a swell of wicked whispers.

I'm sick of being such an abnormal freak. Everything about me is completely weird. How I dress, how I act, how I think.... For instance, I look forward to cuddling up with my biology textbook at night. What teenager in their right mind *likes* that? What's wrong with me?!

I wasn't always such a loser. Would you believe back in the day, I was Miss Popular? Catching lightning bugs with my neighborhood buddies, directing lemonade stands to raise money for cancer, searching for dinosaur bones in the back yard.... I had play dates out the kazoo! Around four years ago, my pool of friends slowly trickled away. They grew interested in make-up, fashion, music stars—glitzy crap that never appealed to me in the slightest. It's as if I'm missing some essential chunk of my cerebrum. Now, my ruler is my only friend, and I feel like I'm missing out on a "normal" high school experience.

I pass the mailbox and a blonde, blue-eyed ball of energy nearly plows me over with a razor scooter. "Catherine!" Little Lexy pulls me into the biggest bear hug he can manage. "I missed you! Did you have a good day at high school today?"

I drop my bag and swing him around in a circle, "I missed you, too, bud! How was your spelling quiz today?" Thank God I have such a sweetheart brother to kiss the frown off my face each afternoon.

It's a typical Tuesday night in the Starkey household. Everybody has something different going on. Mom's busy cleaning out the van from an afternoon of shuffling kids from activity to activity. Between Eli's swim team, Lex's basketball game, my tennis, and Lydia's horseback riding lesson (which requires three round-trips because Lydia always manages to forget something), we live in the car. We ate dinner on the road because Lex was starving at 5 pm when his ADHD pill wore off. When Lex is hungry, Lex must eat. Doctor's orders, we've got to put some meat on his bony butt. It looked like a tornado struck after we raided the McDonalds—empty bags, greasy wrappers, half eaten chicken nuggets, and leaking ketchup packets times a million.

Lydia's in the freezer picking peanut butter cups out of the Moose Tracks ice cream. She's taking a break from her important iChat conversation on Facebook. Usually we ignore each other, but tonight I think I'll step into the target zone and throw out a "How's it going Lydia?"

Cold glare. "Freak." She steps on my toe, plugs in her iTouch earphones, and crawls back into her cave.

"Why do I even try?" I mutter to myself. Lydia and I are as different as chalk and cheese.

"Lydia! I asked you to get off that damn Facebook two hours ago!" Mom half-heatedly scolds, carrying in an armload of junk from the car and kicking the back door shut behind her. "Pick up a book! Stare at the wall! Just get off the computer before I throw it out the window!"

Lydia sits, unmovable, feet cocked up on her desk, completely indifferent. I can feel Mom's heart sink as she ties up the trash bag. She works unbelievably hard to ensure each of us four kids reach our full potential, and it pains me to see her sincere efforts crushed by the immaturity of the ignorant teen.

After quickly cleaning up the kitchen, Mom pours herself a brimming bowl of Captain Crunch topped with peanut butter and settles next to me on the sofa. We never miss the O'Reilly Factor on FOX news. I look forward to bonding with Mom over politics each night; she's the one person I feel like I can talk to.

Tonight's breaking story is about Captain Sullenberger, who miraculously landed a US Airways Airbus on the Hudson River after striking a flock of geese after takeoff. Since Mom has her private pilot's license, she's particularly interested in the details of the story.

"George, good show on FOX!" she beacons Dad, also a piloting enthusiast, to take a break from his studies.

Watching the news report, my mind begins to wander. "How old do you have to be to get a pilot's license anyway?"

"Sixteen solo, seventeen license," Mom tersely replies, concentrating on the flashback showing the plane gliding over the river.

"Wow, that's incredibly earlier than I thought." I consider my sixteenth birthday quickly approaching in the summer. Mom and Dad always rave about how exciting flight is, but I simply don't have what it takes to be a pilot. I'm a joke when it comes to operating machinery, my geography skills are horrendous (I just recently learned that Ohio does not in fact border the Pacific

Ocean), I'm a wimp when it comes to heights....

"Regina, you think Catherine's ready yet?" Dad turns towards Mom.

"Ready for what?" I question, not sure I want to know the answer.

"Well, we always thought you'd want to take flying lessons someday...after we've had so much fun with it...you meet people."

My thumping heart jumps into my throat. Do they seriously think *I* am capable of flying a plane?! Chewing over the idea, I weigh the pros and cons. The only con I can come up with is fear, and unfortunately Mom and Dad have taught me well that being afraid is no excuse to reject a challenge. I gulp, "How would I start?"

Suddenly the fate of the 155 passengers on Airbus A320 seems trivial. Fireworks explode in their eyes and they proceed to enlighten me about the world of flight. Mom immediately calls Burlington Aviation to set up a Discovery Flight at BUY airport.

"This will be the most fun you will ever have. You are so lucky!" she assures me.

It's hard to focus on logarithm homework as my mind churns this novel idea that I am going to fly. In the air. Very soon. Half of my brain says, "No way, this is never going to work out. *Pshhh*, I can't work an iPod let alone pilot a plane." But the other half of me remembers my favorite quote by Eleanor Roosevelt, "Do one thing each day that scares you." This flying business should cover me for a year!

By 9:30, my homework, daily SAT work pages, and piano practice are complete. I tiptoe into the den to kiss Mom goodnight. The sounds of beeping video games, Facebook message alerts, and FOX put me to sleep like a baby.

The day of my Discovery Flight, I anticipate it all day long and hardly seem to notice the usual cheerlessness of the exhausting school day. Mom is first on the pick-up line to drive me out to BUY directly after school. Her fingers tap anxiously on the steering wheel as she pulls around the corner; I've never seen her so excited in all my fifteen years.

"Ready, hun?" Her eyes sparkle and I can't help but smile despite the butterflies in my stomach.

"Yeah, I think so." I throw my heavy load into the trunk. "I hope I love it as much as you do."

I anxiously eye the speedometer pushing past eighty as we race down I-40.

We arrive at the airport, and I'm immediately engulfed in fumes of jet fuel and the loud cranking of engines.

"Your instructor's name is Chris. He's an excellent pilot, and young, so you'll have fun." Mom slings her purse over her shoulder and leads the way into the flight school, a wide grin plastered on her face.

Shy, I follow close behind; half wishing I could turn back.

Eddy, the receptionist at the front desk, greets us, "Howdy, there. You must be our new pilot, Catherine?"

His warm welcome soothes my tension, at least a little. "Ye-yes. Hello. I'm here for my Discovery Flight."

While Mom signs a bunch of waivers and pays the bill, I try to distract my fears by examining the details of the place. Perhaps the most interesting ornaments are the maps covering the walls. I've never seen such confusing maps! Hundreds of symbols, lines, colors, and shades make them practically illegible! My heart rate kicks up a notch.

After what seems like decades, Mom finishes the forms and my instructor arrives.

"Meet Chris, our most renowned instructor at BUY. He'll be taking you up on this beautiful afternoon," Eddy introduces.

Trembling, I shake his hand, and he leads me out the back door towards the hangers. "Have you ever flown before?" Chris questions.

At this point I am about to pee in my pants. A faint "no" is all my stomach can handle. I wave goodbye to Mom, cross my fingers, and resort to deep breathing techniques.

Chris guides me to a Cessna 152, a high wing two-seater. After conducting a careful pre-flight inspection, we assume our seats in the plane, buckle up, and taxi towards the end of runway 24.

He hands me a set of enormous headsets, and I fumble to fix them over my ponytail. "Plug them in here."

My jaw gapes open in awe at his swiftness and ease in manipulating all the gadgets on the dashboard. "Talk about multi-tasking," I attempt to ease my tenseness.

"I've been flying for longer than you've been alive. I know this plane better than the back of my hand." Chris taxis the plane effortlessly with his big toe. As we near the end of the runway he says, "So, how'd you like to take us up on your own?"

"Are you nuts?!" I blurt out, panicked. I can't work an oven let alone work a plane.

"Calm down, now, take it easy," Chris reasons. "I wouldn't let you do anything I don't think is safe. Just follow my instructions, okay?"

I hyperventilate slightly, and in the spur of the moment agree to direct the plane in takeoff. Chris aims the nose directly down the runway with his fancy footwork, and continues, "It's simple now, really. I want you to push the throttle in all the way and hold it there—don't let go—then, when this green line hits fifty-five, slowly pull back." He lifts my hand and positions it on the throttle.

Baboom, baboom, baboom, now my heart has moved from my throat into my ears.

"Just push it in...all the way...and hold it there."

"Push it in and hold it there?"

"That's right."

"And pull back at fifty-five? At fifty-five?"

"That's right"

"Okay."

"Okey-dokey, whenever you're ready." Chris tosses the pre-flight checklist over his shoulder into the trunk.

A century rolls by before I finally muster up the courage to push in the throttle. The engine roars, the propeller whirls, the whole plane vibrates like a threshing machine, and we begin to pick up speed down the runway. I concentrate all my energy on the green arrow, worried I'll forget to start pulling when it hits the line.

"Forty, forty-five, fifty..." I whisper.

Soon we are off the ground and soaring up into the sky! Chris takes the controls and I hold onto my seatbelt and polyester seat for dear life. Simultaneously, I gaze out the window at the glory of the earth and sky working together to create a masterpiece of grandeur.

We tilt left-crosswind. "Whoa," I exclaim as gravity tugs me into the window. We climb higher and higher, and Chapel Hill shrinks into a cluster of dollhouses and scampering ants. My fear melts away and I embrace the wonder of flight!

Chris points into the distance, "Ya know what that mountain is?"

I squint at the cone-shaped protuberance with a uniquely naked apex. "You're asking the wrong person."

Chris chuckles. "It's Pilot Mountain. A crucial landmark for us pilots. It's located precisely on the VOR 46 course."

"Oh, that name's familiar. We drive past there on the way to visit my grandparents," I mention, although I'm sure Chris doesn't really care about my family vacations. I never understood why it was called "Pilot Mountain." To non-pilots, Pilot Mountain holds little, if any, significance at all. But for sky-goers, the mountain is apparently a critical key in pinpointing your location—a lifeline.

"Interesting," I silently conclude to myself.

We loop around the billowing clouds and I notice individual rays of sunlight emanating in isolated black streaks from beneath. It's a whole different world. Below, Chapel Hill is merely one of the beads along the string that is the Interstate. In the cities, thousands of people, together with the homes and shopping centers, homogenize into a panorama of green dappled with flakes of gray.

My focus drifts away from the cities to the checkered farmland. Each individual farm is neatly cultivated and clearly separate from the rest. The plowed fields and winding country roads work together to define the geometrical design. *The land is so organized*, I think to myself.

Every ounce of worry, fear, and distress in my life evaporates. In the brilliance of the sun, it is simply impossible to think worrisome thoughts. A sense of peace overcomes me, and I feel a comfort indescribable with words. It hits me how very miniscule my life is. The place I thought I occupied in this world is turned upside down; more literally, it is put to flight.

As he maneuvers the plane, Chris points out important places familiar to me on the ground. "That's the RBC Center...and over there's the Durham Bulls baseball stadium."

From a bird's eye view, the places are totally unfamiliar to me. I get a better perspective of the layout of the buildings and their position in Chapel Hill as a whole. It is impossible to locate East Chapel Hill High hidden somewhere in the forests of loblolly pines and masses of cookie-cutter houses.

Without a doubt, Mom was absolutely correct in that the Discovery Flight is by far the most exhilarating and eye-opening experience of my life. Nothing can wipe the grin off my face, not even evil Lydia. Overwhelmed with a sense of pride and accomplishment, I ponder, *Wonder how the fashion gurus and gangsta crowd at East would handle this.*

When I arrive home, Lex gallops towards me, jumps into my arms, and gives me a big wet kiss on the nose. "Hey, bud! It's good to see you too!" I giggle.

I settle on the sofa and flick on FOX. Mom prepares a cup of joe before hurrying in to join me. *Super Mario Brothers* and Lydia's cell phone buzz from the computer room and Lex burns marshmallows on the kitchen stove. I pull out my Latin textbook from under the sofa cushion and think to myself, "Boy, am I glad that some things never change."

Faithful sunshine floods my bedroom; I pull on a hoodie and

sneak out the back door for my morning run. I appreciate the loblollies, tenaciously holding their color through the unrelenting season. The rooftops sparkle with frost lace and sparrows weave figure eights around the block, anticipating spring.

"Wait up, Cathy." Juliana targets me in the hallway.

I leaf through my biology binder; "Here, I already made you a copy."

"Oh, thanks." An awkward smile spreads across her face.

My watch beeps and I make my way to English class.

"Cathy Starkey," Ms. Pernell mumbles.

"Present." I thumb through the pages to last night's assignment and pull out the pen in my front pocket.

Wonder what good ole Odysseus will grapple with next?

About the author:

Regina is an eleventh-grade student at The Lawrenceville School in New Jersey. Writing has been her passion since she was seven years old and exchanging letters with the Tooth Fairy. In 2005, she published her children's book "Let Freedom Ring" through the charity Kids DOnate, Inc. More recently, Regina earned three Gold Key awards in the National Alliance for Young Writers competition, and first prize in essay contests sponsored by the National Center for Science Education, the American Institute of Certified Public Accountants (AICPA), and the American Legion of NC. In 2009, Regina co-authored a scientific research paper during an internship in WIL Research Laboratories.

When she's not writing, Regina stays busy playing Varsity tennis, running, tracking politics, and leading an active Red Cross club at her boarding school. A certified single-engine private pilot, Regina adores flying—except when there are thunderstorms in the vicinity.

HE DOES THE BEST HE CAN
©2011 by Simone Hanson

A one-armed chickadee is as good as dead; it can't be expected to survive a Maine winter. That was my argument and my father agreed. I'd found the bird hopping frantically on top of ice crusted snow one morning, skipping in foolish circles, unable to navigate on the ground with only one working wing. I'd chased him around, trying to be careful, but my boots punching through the icy crust of snow must have sounded like the end of the world to him, and when he finally tipped over the edge of a footprint and disappeared entirely into the powdery snow beneath, he must have thought he'd fallen off the edge of the earth. So he seemed pretty grateful by the time I got him in the house.

My mother took one look at him and said, "Celeste, put that thing back outside." She said it was crazy to keep a wild bird in a cage for the rest of its life, it was unnatural. She asked my father why he had to keep encouraging me.

"What do you want me to do, wring its neck?" he asked her and she gave him one of her looks. But she went down to the cellar and came up with a rusted bird cage that we'd saved from our parakeet days.

We kept the bird in his little cage and he seemed to enjoy all the attention he got. We kept him by the door so he could see outside whenever anyone opened it and I always got the impression he was happy. He was curious and attentive, and he ended up surviving for more than a year, a lot longer than we expected.

Nevertheless, my mother always made a cooing noise whenever she went near his cage and addressed him as "poor little thing." He'd look at her, his tiny head held sideways, eyes blinking, like he didn't know whom she could possibly be talking about.

He died on a late spring day, on my brother's birthday to be exact, which was a bad omen. And unnecessary, since we all pretty much knew my brother wasn't going to have a good time anyway. Peter's birthdays were never good, never higher than our lowest expectations. My mother said it was because he was a Wednesday child, born full of woe. His birthdays were a constant reminder of how life can—and will—throw you curve balls just for the fun of it.

He was nine that year, and it was supposed to be his last blow-out party since we stopped with the extravaganzas when we hit double digits, but this year Peter's birthday fell one week after our aunt's funeral and my mother didn't think it was appropriate to have a party. I think she was fairly well done with parties by then anyway and what better excuse than a death in the family?

So, the newly widowed Uncle Romeo was coming over instead, which really wasn't vastly better than a bunch of little boys filling the house. My uncle could make the air freeze. But he was alone now, again. "Third time through the wringer," was how my father put it, shaking his head at the specter of losing three wives in one life time. Really, there was no escaping the duty to make sure he wasn't alone on the very first Sunday after this last blow.

On the morning of the big day, it rained of course. It started in torrents; the kind of storm that intends to run itself out quickly, like it maybe has something better to do later. It left behind a misty wet grayness hanging in the air and pools of brown mud in the yard.

"It's a good thing you're not having a party this year," my mother said. "Imagine having all those children in the house."

"Yeah. I'd be miserable."

Peter's specialty was deadpan sarcasm. He was only nine but already learning to take disappointment in stride. It's a good trait to have, this ability to look at injuries like each one is a bad pitch, then moving out of the way, and tracking it to the catcher's mitt. He just steps back up to the plate and waits patiently with the bat on his shoulder, never doubting that once in a while something will sail right in his zone and he'll be able to take a swing.

They were in the kitchen. Peter was helping her make his own birthday cake because when he was really little he loved baking and so she thought he still did. Once my mother got something in her head, it was stuck there, frozen solid. She had him grating hazelnuts and was telling him to hurry since it was already late afternoon and she hadn't gotten her cake in the oven yet.

Peter sat at the counter, his long legs dangling from the stool, his blue eyes focused on my mother's new food processor. My mother never made the same birthday cake twice since she thought we needed to start out each new year of our lives with some variety. Of the choices she'd given him, he'd picked a hazelnut cake because he wanted to use the Cuisinart, which everybody loved like it was the newest member of the family. The circular grater buzzed around fast as light, making a zipping sound whenever he pushed a small nut through. He was grating them one at a time, mesmerized by his power to send a hard object through the blade, spinning it into dust particles like a small explosion.

The smell of pot roast and cake had just started colliding when Uncle Romeo announced his arrival with a hard fist against the metal storm door, hacking a few seconds off our lives. My mother made a sharp ticking sound, and my father said he'd get it, reaching for the door and pushing it open a little too fast and wide. Uncle Romeo swung off the front steps, knuckles white from gripping the door handle. We watched, unblinking, as he arced like a pendulum back to a standing position and then swung smoothly into the house.

"Easy, Cap'n," he said to my father as he slapped him on the back. "Almost knocked the old man off the stoop." He always called him Captain. Decades earlier, as a senior in high school, my father had been captain of the hockey team and Uncle Romeo never really got over it, he was so proud. My father could have become an arsonist and Uncle Romeo would still have thought humanity began with his younger brother.

As for himself, he was a caricature of a man, all head and slight body. His eyes were chronically bloodshot and rheumy and his fingers were drawn to them, always digging. He had an aquiline nose, the elegance marred by the veins that stretched across it, throbbing in time to some secret music. He had two tiny pinprick scars right above his lip. When I was little, I used to kneel on his lap to get a good look. "Kissed a snake," he'd explain. "Wouldn't recommend it."

My mother always said those scars were from getting his mouth stapled shut one time.

Uncle Romeo was the head of maintenance down at the cemetery. Don't ask me why, but there was something about dead people that attracted him. While all the guys who worked for him might have made sure the graves were kept nice for the families who visited the sites, Uncle Romeo seemed to think he worked for those who lay beneath. He told me once he didn't like that the dead could only be forgotten.

They became his acquaintances—his friends even—and when Uncle Romeo would tell his stories, it felt as though he'd just had dinner with them. "Oh yes, they love me over there," he'd often say, and I knew he referred to the dead and buried, not the guys who worked for him.

"I thought you weren't working today, Romeo," my mother said, eyeing the wet boots he had forgotten to remove. He was wearing his green cemetery uniform, his name stitched in red script across the shirt pocket, done in such intricate embroidery you really had to know the name in order to be able to read it.

"Had an emergency," he burst out, his voice shocking, too big for his stature. He always started talking like he'd been waiting a million years for someone to finally ask him something.

"They called me in; on my day off, of all days. If you can believe that. But what can you do when you're the prime caretaker? You heard about that old woman died last week? In that car wreck? Got hit by two cars at the same time? Gotta be a real bad driver have that happen to you. Blind-as-a-bat the last five years, shouldn't of been driving. Whole family said so. She's the LaPointe family, though. Or was. Heh! Guess there's no telling someone of that caliber she's not driving anymore. Not unless you want out of the will. That's what the nephew mentioned."

He stopped talking briefly, like he'd hit a rest stop on a music score. We took the opportunity to sit down at the table with him, except my mother. She continued to move around the kitchen, anxious to get dinner on the table, but her eyes kept darting toward us from across the counter that divided the kitchen from the dining room, always a sucker for gossip.

"We had a grave already dug up for her over by the rest of the family. But evidently, she had it in her will she wanted to be buried off by herself, under some tree that faces the rising sun. Some dingleberry thing about being the first to catch the morning rays. They recited this god-awful poem at the gravesite—the new one that I had to dig this morning. In...the...rain, thank you very much. Couldn't of told anyone in advance, oh no, that would be too convenient."

We hunkered down around the table, watching him with the same enthusiasm we might feel for a television show we liked well enough but wasn't our favorite, or maybe a rerun, a script gone stale because we already knew the ending. He told us his own personal theory for old Mrs. LaPointe's final instructions. He figured she'd had a thing with Mr. Conte, who was buried right across from the new site. Mr. Conte had been her mechanic...and do not ask me what he thought they'd been doing right before he died of a massive coronary.

My father said he might not want to mention that too loudly at the cemetery.

"What? She gonna sue me? She's dead for Christ sake."

My mother made her ticking sound again and my father did not look at her but steered the course of the conversation off in another direction. "So. You doing okay, Romeo? Getting along all right?"

"Oh sure, sure. I've been here before you know. I'm used to being alone. I fix a good meal now and then, watch some TV. I'm doing good."

I guess he would be used to widowhood by now. Uncle Romeo buried wives like...well, like a gravedigger, I suppose. He wore them out, that's what my mother said. They were worn down to the treads after just a few years, having to traverse rougher terrain than most women.

"Well, you just relax, take it easy," my father told him. "You need anything? A cup of coffee?"

"Sure, that would be nice. Warm me up a little. Still got the cold rain in my bones from this morning." He smiled at Peter as my brother got up to get the coffee pot. I slid the cream and sugar over toward Uncle Romeo's end of the table as my mother set the cauldron of pot roast down. Uncle Romeo leaned back, hands behind his neck, smiling like mankind had finally reached world peace. He bowed his head and kept silent as we said a quick prayer.

Listening to him as he knit together more stories for us, I felt something pressing against the back of my eyes. I wanted to ask something about Aunt Jackie, the most recent cause of his widowhood. She had been my favorite aunt so far and I was afraid of ignoring her absence. I wanted to ask how he was getting along without her, without her unparalleled lasagna, the Saturday Night Special. Was he taking care of their dog? Was he going to repaint the house this summer, like she'd planned on doing? She had been a lightning bolt, highly charged and full of light, and I wondered how he was handling the darkness that must have settled around him. But I couldn't think how to ask and I let the moment slip past.

"Hey! Are we forgetting about the birthday boy?" Uncle Romeo snapped his attention in my brother's direction. He reached out to pound Peter on the shoulder. "Peter Daniel Au Claire. Nine years old all of a sudden. I remember when I used to change your diapers."

That's another thing about Uncle Romeo. He liked to start conversations with conversation stoppers. Peter's eyes went haywire, not knowing how to escape. But Uncle Romeo was turning wistful. Every sentence started with 'I remember when...', like he was writing a ballad. And, of course, we all had to chime in. I agreed that Peter's was the cutest baby butt in the world and he made a point of reminding everyone of my lead in the sixth-grade math play.

And so we talked. We went all the way back to my parent's wedding and the best-man toast Uncle Romeo made at the reception, the one that even made their father start crying. We made him feel that we wanted to know everything he had to say, because we wanted him to be happy when he was at our house. And because he made us feel virtuous, like we were tithing, sacrificing little pieces of ourselves for his sake. My father said it was important, that he needed us because he didn't have anyone else left. Not really. Not if you don't count dead people.

It was because when he was young, and not ready for it, Uncle Romeo had been hit with disappointment. He'd been a hockey player in high school, and a good one. The best goalie in the high school league, according to my father. And when he was a senior, word got out that the Bruins were sending a scout up from Boston. The general opinion was that the Bruins were playing on cracked ice, had been for a few years, and they needed new blood. "They were coming for Romeo, everyone knew it. That's how good he was."

And for Guy LaMare. The two of them, fierce opponents, were the league stand-outs, Romeo for his fearless defense of the goal, and LaMare for his sheer skill and legendary strength. Together, they were the Paul Bunyons of youth hockey.

But in the third game of his final season, Romeo stopped one goal that he should have let pass. They could have made a movie out of it, the way he blocked every shot with the skill of a pro, playing way beyond his years, way beyond anyone else on the ice. Except for his only real opponent, Guy LaMare, who took his final shot like he was firing a cannon.

The crowd almost brought the roof down when he failed to score, but went dead silent when they noticed their goalie wasn't moving. Romeo had taken the puck right between the eyes and it took him down. He was out for several seconds before making his shaken way out of the rink, to a standing ovation. My father always told the story like he didn't think we'd really believe him, or that we couldn't possibly understand the roar of the crowd that was like thunder, so loud that he clung to his mother, thinking the trembling bleachers were going to cave in.

The next week, a scout from Boston really did come up. Romeo wasn't on the ice because his eyes were still swollen shut and he hadn't gotten his balance back, and so the Bruins lost what may have been the best goalie they ever had. They did sign Guy LaMare, though. At first, he refused because he felt so bad about Romeo, felt responsible for what happened to him, and didn't feel right leaving him behind. But in the end, he signed and he played for a few years before returning home after a bad knee injury. He went to work for a bank downtown and my parents got their mortgage from him.

Uncle Romeo never fully recovered from the crushing injuries to his face. His eyes gave him trouble for the rest of his life, and his brain, once it settled back down in his skull, settled into a different place. He wasn't fast anymore. Didn't think fast, didn't move fast. It was as though a big hole had opened up in front of him, and he wasn't quick enough to run around it before the dark mouth gaped too wide, and he stumbled into it. The farther down he went, the higher the walls reached until he couldn't quite see over the top, and he couldn't get out. So he ended up working at the biggest cemetery in the city right after he graduated; so big it has a lake in the middle of it and woods that surround it. It's practically a nature preserve and Uncle Romeo complains a lot about the woodchucks who dig holes better than he does.

When supper was finished and the stories were told, we sat for a while, quiet, not sure how to get back to the present. It had started getting dark in the house. Scraping his chair across the floor, my father got up and suggested taking a little air before having cake and ice cream.

"I've got a tree to show you, Romeo. Tell me what you think I should do. There's a branch hanging over the house I don't like the look of. Got hit by lightening last year and now it's hanging by a thread. Falls off, I'll need a new roof."

"I'll see what I can do, Cap'n," he said, grabbing Peter by the shoulders and telling him to come along with the men.

OK, there was no way Uncle Romeo was going to have a helpful opinion about that tree. The last time my father asked him for help, we ended up needing a new dishwasher. And that wasn't the only avoidable disaster we'd experienced. But my father would let Uncle Romeo decimate every appliance in the house if he thought it might do him some good.

"He does the best he can," he'd say each time Uncle Romeo left the house, his rusted, maroon Pontiac rumbling happily down the street as he headed home, leaving something broken or hurt in his wake.

I had to wonder, though, whether my father would really put a chainsaw in his hands and tell him it was all right to take down a tree.

My mother was thinking the same thing. "If that tree comes through the roof of this house, I'll have his head on a plate, I mean it."

I wasn't quite sure whose head she was talking about. It could have been either one.

The rain was a thin mist and the three of them came back in the house about a half hour later, looking damp and dreary, wearing the weather on their faces. Uncle Romeo was saying the next time he had a day off he'd be over to help with the tree. My mother's back straightened so rigidly, I swear I could hear it crack.

Cake and coffee were on the table, as well as a small pile of presents. Nine candles glowed on the cake and Peter took them off so my mother could cut it. Uncle Romeo asked what kind of cake it was, jabbing a piece with his fork. He spit it out on his plate just as I told him it was a German hazelnut cake. It was a good thing he didn't swallow it.

He bolted to his feet, his face contorted, eyes bulging. "I'm allergic," he wheezed, just as his throat closed up.

We all just watched him, gawking in breathless awe, like he was putting on a one-man show. We didn't even notice my mother eventually rush from the table and launch herself into the kitchen, we were so engrossed in the golf ball welts that were popping out all over his face and neck. She returned with a red box in her hands, which she tore open as she ran, telling Uncle Romeo to stay calm. She pulled out a syringe and a small glass bottle.

Luckily for Uncle Romeo, my mother was allergic to bees. It was truly heroic, the way she plunged the needle into his leg as calmly as sticking a meat thermometer into a duck. I wouldn't have guessed she had it in her.

All at once, Uncle Romeo's breathing resumed, though labored and rasping, and he slowly let himself fall back into the chair. His head was one giant red welt and he kept desperately scratching his face and neck like he was fighting off fire ants. "Who in the hell makes cakes with hazelnuts?" he finally managed. "Jesus!"

"It's common in Germany," my father informed him. "You know Marie grew up in Germany, right?" He sounded like a professor starting a history lesson. The absurdity stopped him and he put his arm awkwardly across Uncle Romeo's shoulders and asked him if he was all right, did he want to go to the hospital? Because he'd take him. Right now.

We all stared, waiting for Uncle Romeo to tell us he was good, nothing had ever kept him down for long and would we all stop staring at him and get him something to eat that didn't have any goddamned hazelnuts in it? We waited for him to take a swig from the flask we all knew he kept in his back pocket for emergencies. Instead, he looked at each of us, one by one, his eyes—at least what we could see of them—clearer than I'd ever seen them. Bright in fact, like sunshine glancing off the water.

He hesitated. "Can I stay? Do you think I could stay here? Till tomorrow? Just in case I have a relapse, you know?"

My mother was quick to tell him that wouldn't happen but that it might be a good idea to get checked out. "Frank can drive you to the emergency room and then he'll take you home. You'll be fine."

The tenor of her voice was meant to call him back, to get the old Romeo to come out of hiding and this scared version to disappear. But instead, he broke down completely. With shaking hands, he wiped at his swollen eyes. "If I die, I don't want to die alone."

None of us believed for a second that he was going to die. In fact, his head was already slowly shrinking and he breathed more easily. But he had come pretty close, we didn't doubt it, so who were we to say how he should feel? My mother said she'd get blankets and make up the couch, unless he wanted Peter's bed.

"No, couch is good," he said softly. Even if his face didn't look like he'd spent the last two weeks underwater, he would still have been unrecognizable. Fear or dread, whatever had hold of him, had changed him. He was quiet and his eyes were desperate. It was like looking at the wrong side of the moon.

My mother said, "Whatever you want, Romeo. Whatever you want." Her hand on his shoulder was warm and steady.

Hours later, the house was quiet and dark, except for the yellow glow from the streetlight that streaked its way into my room, cutting through a thick fog that moved around the house like a quiet animal. It had been an odd day, something to file away for a while and pull out when I needed a good story. But that night, I couldn't sleep, thinking about Uncle Romeo's near miss. Our near loss. It's all so quick and strange, and my heart was pounding in my head, thinking how fast everything can fall away and leave us just free-falling, pinwheeling in the rushing air, never knowing where we're going to land.

It's times like these that you start thinking of every bad thing that has ever happened. I had no deep tragedies of my own at the time but I wasn't ready to let go of this ethereal feeling of dread yet, so I drifted back a few years to another story, one that had gripped the city with all the intensity of a real-life Hansel and Gretel tale. Lovely in its sadness.

Two children had gone missing, a boy and his little sister. There they were, playing in the yard one minute, gone the next. Search parties had made way for bloodhounds, and the dogs had tracked them over a mile through dense woods, to the edge of a quarry. In the desperate search to find them, the quarry had been drained. Over two million gallons of water had to be pumped out, and when it was empty, the police found more than what they were looking for. They found the children. They also found several old bicycles, three cars, and a washing machine. There was a dead woman whose body had been caught on the craggy edge of the quarry wall, and the skeletal remains of a man, dead maybe twenty years by the coroner's estimate, was found resting on the murky bottom. There was a whole world down there, a world of people, pets, toys, old tools and household junk. All kinds of debris that had floated down from the real world to form this new one. What had been emptied and ruined was recreated. A defiant rejoinder of the wronged and discarded.

The story of these children had been in the papers every day, it was the biggest tragedy the state had ever known. **LOST AND FOUND!** the papers had declared, right above their school pictures and photos of their bewildered parents. Sympathy for the parents poured in like buckets of sand, burying them under piles of letters and lilies. But I couldn't stop thinking of those children, and how the parents should have watched out for them better, not leaving it up to the world to keep them out of trouble. This isn't a fairy tale we're living in, I wanted to tell them. Bread crumbs weren't going to lead them home.

These children, these lost and found children, haunted me that night. They got me out of bed and I wandered through the dark house, sleep plagued, believing I could help them retrace their steps and bring them back. But on this night, all I could do was remember another time I wandered down the hall, a still night nine years ago. An image. Peter was just born, my parents measuring his life in hours. My mother was exhausted and my father had recruited Uncle Romeo to help.

"I can do it, I know I can do it," he'd assured my mother, the same way an excited teenager might argue he's ready to drive a car. "Christ sake, I can hold a baby," he'd said in response to her doubtful face. "Go on, get some rest."

And in the darkness of that night, nine years ago, I could hear the soft creaking of the rocking chair, the soft crying of a baby who is giving in to sleep, and my uncle singing. He was singing Danny Boy, over and over, his soft thread of a voice binding all the assurances of love together tightly, as tightly as a promise. A promise that nothing would ever come completely undone, never be entirely lost or left empty.

About the author:

Simone Hanson lives just outside Atlanta with her husband, three boys and two dogs. She is a former school administrator and lawyer but left the working world to stay home with her children because she is not the supermom she thought she was going to be. Now that her children have become fascinated with things other than her, she has turned to writing.A novel, which includes the characters in this short story, is currently being reconstructed. Originally from Maine, her writing is set there as it is the place she knows best. Besides writing, her hobbies include pottery, tennis and dog-walking.

THE RING
©2011 by Denise C. Hengeli

White gold molded into a bow, sprinkled with diamond dust. Simple. Feminine. Inexpensive. Yet, when presented to Sheila, a mixture of unending sadness is brightened by appreciation for this gift from her father.

"Dad! Mom's ring? For me? I thought you'd wait until I was older." Pushing the ring onto her finger, Sheila recalls the scent of her mother's favorite powder. "As though she's hugging me."

"You're so much like your mother, you bring me comfort, Sheila," Marvin sighs. "Have her ring. It's beautiful on your hand. I'm going out for a walk for a little while."

Sheila sees *MAG* etched inside the ring. "Maggie Agnes Grembling," she whispers. "Quite a name, eh, Dad? Quite a lady." Sheila hugs her father. "Have a good walk, Dad. Come back soon, it's cold out."

His daughter's hug doesn't lessen Marvin's sadness. His bent head defines total disinterest in his surroundings as he walks down three steps to the front walk of his forty-year-old house. Three houses past his own, he sits heavily on a neighborhood bench. "There isn't any place I want to go. Nothing interests me. I'll sit here for a while so Sheila can enjoy her present."

Not wanting to witness her father's sadness, Sheila enters the living room and sits in her mother's reclining chair. She turns the ring around her finger, remembering the past two years. On Sheila's twenty-fifth birthday, Maggie became pre-occupied with the idea that her daughter should get a mammogram. She reminded Sheila of the family's propensity for breast cancer.

"I'm too young for a mammogram, Mom. Really!"

Once introduced, the subject was discussed daily. Magazine clippings were shared between the women, detailing statistics of the recurrence of family breast cancers.

"I don't have time now, Mom. It's too far to go. I'd be embarrassed. It'll hurt." Each objection was countered with stories of relatives, neighbors, and casual friends who battled cancer.

"I'll go with you," Maggie promised. "I'll wait right outside for you. It's important to me that you go."

One Monday night Marvin watched football as the women talked about the now familiar subject. "Why are you two quibbling?" Sheila's father asked. "Who's trying to convince whom of what and why?"

"Mom wants me to have a mammogram, but I'm too young, Dad. Besides, it's too far to go. I'll be embarrassed.

I'm afraid," Sheila admitted.

"The last reason sounds the most **probable**," Sheila's father snorted. "Why? Does it hurt?"

"Marvin, it's only an X-ray seeking cancer. There's a little squashing of breast tissue, but it's really not painful."

"Wait! Cancer?" Marvin was suddenly interested and clearly alarmed.

"Relax. It's not that I think Sheila has it, but you know your sister had it a while back."

"Oh, yeah. That. She's a lot older than Sheila though." Marvin's attention returned to the football game. Mother and daughter rolled their eyes at Marvin's shift of interest.

"How often do you get a mammogram, Mom?"

"Me? Oh, I never get them."

"You've never had one? And, you want me to go? I can't believe this. I won't get one unless you get one too."

"Oh, for goodness sakes. O.K. I'll get one if that will get you to the clinic. But, I don't need one. It's your dad's side of the family that has had cancer."

Again switching his attention, Marvin said, "Go, Maggie. You can't get sick. Who'll make Sunday dinner if you get sick?" Maggie took off her slipper and threw it across the room at her husband. "I'm kidding, I'm kidding," Marvin squalled, returning his attention to football.

Sheila folded her arms across her chest as though to protect herself from further scrutiny and sighed, "Make the appointment, Mom. We'll go next week."

As Sheila recalls the conversation, she settles deeper into the recliner as a shield from her memories. She always relied on her mother's company, preferring her to other family members, friends, or neighbors. They seemed shallow in comparison. She knew her mother's ideas before they were verbalized using the abbreviated language of familiarity, mother and daughter completing each other's sentences without surprise or apology. They were so similar, people couldn't tell which was mother and which was daughter, much to Maggie's delight. They walked with matching gaits, enjoyed shopping, selected matching outfits without intent. No facet of their life was private from the other. They were friend-friend, female-female, mother-daughter. They complained about their weight and daily planned to lose fifteen pounds.

Now alone, Sheila remembers the smell of fresh pink paint that covered the walls of the cancer prevention center. There were no empty chairs in the waiting room filled with bored-looking people. Men sat holding large, black purses, over-stuffed with papers and pictures their wives carried. Their faces were lined with concern over body parts that used to bring pleasure but had turned to parts for worry. Each swing of an inner clinic door presented a woman searching the room for the familiar face of her husband. When their eyes met, the men rose, transferring the purse back to their wives as they shuffled out the automatic exit door.

"See, Mom? I'm the youngest woman here," Sheila whispered. "I don't even have a husband to hold my purse."

"Shush," Maggie replied. "You just don't want to be here."

"You've got that right!"

At a window marked *Sign In*, both women were handed blank postcards with instructions to address them to themselves so the clinic could mail them test results.

"Think they could address these themselves," Sheila complained.

"Just do it," Maggie instructed, handing Sheila one of several pens housed in her purse.

As soon as they handed back the postcards they were ushered into an inner room where tiny paper shirts lay on a table. A nurse wearing a white uniform decorated with balloons commanded, "Take a paper shirt, remove everything above your waist, including jewelry and deodorant, and wait for me. There are alcohol pads to clean off any cream or perfume you might be wearing. I'll come get you when you're ready."

"Guess when you wear a uniform you're in charge," Sheila said. "Even if it has balloon decorations."

"Complaints, complaints," said Maggie as she put her arm around Sheila's paper shirt. "Here comes the nurse. See you later."

When the women were finished with their trips to the radiology lab, they met again in the hallway. "Let's get dressed and have some tea," Sheila suggested. "Glad that's over."

They enjoyed fresh fruit with their tea in the cafe next door to the clinic and giggled over the impersonal treatment they received.

"Impersonal it was, but with very personal parts!" Sheila laughed.

Three days later, Sheila was surprised to see her own handwriting on a postcard. Flipping it over, she read that her mammogram results were fine. Sheila called her mother. "Did you get your postcard today?" Sheila asked. "Impersonal to the last. Even the mail carrier knows about the health of my breasts."

"No, mine hasn't arrived yet, dear. Maybe tomorrow's mail."

Returning to daily routines, the next five days passed without concern. Checking her mailbox on the sixth day, Maggie suddenly became frightened when she saw there was still no postcard for her. Why hadn't her card arrived?

Sunday was spent lazily at a local picnic area, but Maggie's thoughts kept returning to her missing postcard. "Tomorrow I'll get it. I'm sure of it."

The next day Maggie was waiting next to the mailbox when the mail carrier greeted, "Good morning!" Handing her a stack of letters he returned to his open van and continued filling curbside mailboxes.

With shaking hands, Maggie sorted white envelopes, silently studying the one with a return address she didn't recognize. Still no postcard. She put the mysterious envelope on the center of her kitchen table as though to touch it would ensure bad news. She boiled eggs for lunch, decided what she'd prepare for dinner, crossed off days on her calendar, put out a new tissue box, decided she needed a manicure, grabbed her car keys, and left her house.

"I feel great," she told herself. "I won't think about it."

Her answering machine was blinking when she returned to her kitchen. Sheila's voice questioned, "Where are you Mom? Pick up the phone. Are you home? Call me."

Maggie knew her daughter would want to know where she had been and why she didn't get invited for a manicure trip, so she made a cup of tea before she returned the call. "Hey, kiddo," she said gaily. "What's up?"

"Hey, Mom. Where've you been? Did you get your postcard yet?"

The question Maggie most wanted to avoid opened Sheila's conversation. "Went to fill my gas tank. The dashboard light came on yesterday."

"Did you get your postcard yet?"

"The mail's not here yet," Maggie lied. I'll call you when it gets here. Talk to you later."

Somehow menacing, the white envelope seemed bigger than it was. Maggie pulled it towards her, slit the top open,and let the paper lay before her. "This is silly," she thought. "It's probably from a marketing company offering credit cards."

Opening the tri-folded paper she read, *Please get in touch with this office to review your mammogram results.* Tears blurred her vision as the letter continued, *Images dictate further review.*

"I think I knew. I really knew." Maggie rested her head on the table as silent tears wet her face. She was still resting on the table when Sheila opened the kitchen door and chirped, "Hey, Mom. Did your postcard come?"

"No, dear. Just this letter."

Searching her mother's face, Sheila was immediately alarmed. She snatched the letter, drew in her breath, and sat heavily onto a kitchen chair. "Oh, Mom. Medical words always sound bad. This can't be as scary as it sounds. You're healthy, full of energy, and I love you too much for anything bad to happen to you."

Remembering the day so clearly, Sheila squirms deeper into the shelter of the recliner chair. Scenes filled with blurs of doctor visits, hospital stays, slow dripping chemotherapy, hair loss, weight loss, and at the end, never-diminishing pain bring new tears to her eyes. Maggie seemed to vanish, to shrink before Sheila's eyes. Nightly they cried, pleaded, bargained with God, promising to do every good thing, if only Maggie would live. Sheila kept vigil at her mother's bedside but couldn't delay her death. Maggie welcomed death for its release of pain. Sheila held her hand long into the night not knowing how she could possibly tell this beloved woman a final good-bye.

Suddenly, Sheila hears the door open and her father returns to the living room, smiling gently at her. To shake off the memory that engulfs her, Sheila rises from the recliner, still holding one hand over the other to protect the band of white gold encircling her finger.

She tells her father, "I feel better now, Dad. You know, the bond between mother and daughter is never broken. It can't be, since the bond *created* the daughter. It's never good-bye. Think I'll go make two cups of tea, one for me and one for Mom. Would you like to join us?"

Marvin smiles broadly. "That would be fine, Sheila. Just fine. Mother always loved her tea."

About the author:
A graduate of Florida Atlantic University at age sixty-four, Denise is honored by being selected as a finalist in Scribes Valley's 2010 contest. She creates short-stories, children's stories and poetry, and has been published in The Lutheran Digest. A busy grandmother of six, she recently relocated to Atlanta, where she enjoys Southern hospitality. Denise has enjoyed writing fiction for the past twenty years and 'lives to imagine' her work published.

MUSCADINE WINE
©2011 by Sheila White

She felt the sun drop its autumn warmth from around her shoulders as she walked under the bridge. Her brown eyes squinted as they adjusted to the dim light. Walking carefully, stepping over rocks and empty cans, she found him lying in a bundle on a dirty, worn sleeping bag. The noisy sounds from vehicles passing overhead silenced his breathing. Thinking him dead, she held her breath. In a short, quiet lull, she heard a snore. She lowered her backpack from around her neck and a heavy sigh drooped her shoulders. Sitting down next to the filthy man, she studied him as he slept. The small amount of silver hair on his head and face was matted. The stench from his soiled body and tattered clothing was nauseating. Where had the happy, younger man gone?

Everyone remembered him before he forgot. He'd been a vibrant man, a stranger to no one, with a smile that warmed the coldest hearts. He'd had a lifelong weakness for football, golf, and younger women but none of that mattered anymore. He'd forgotten. The sickness gnawed at his brain, always making him forget. Always he wanted to remember. The vultures were just outside, already fighting over the best morsels. He saw them in his dream, flying circles just above his head. He wondered how they knew he was dying. He wondered why they were already coming to feast when he wasn't dead yet. He couldn't remember. But he knew the vultures knew somehow. But he didn't move. He couldn't remember if he should or shouldn't move because of the vultures. But he couldn't remember why. So he lay still.

He hadn't moved or spoken in weeks but as she reached over to touch the thin vein slowly pulsating in his dirty hand, his eyes flashed open and he said, "Would you shut the window please? I feel a cold breeze."

She answered, "Oh, I'm sorry. Yes, let me get the window. Here, I brought you something." After pulling a two-liter bottle filled with muscadine wine from her backpack, she unscrewed the lid and handed the bottle to him. She remembered it was his favorite.

He sat up slowly and reached with a trembling hand. He couldn't remember who she was. Her voice was familiar, but in his head the who was nowhere to be found. He remembered he was thirsty, so he put the container to his dry, cracked lips and swallowed several times. Then he smiled. He welcomed the familiar liquid as it warmed him going down. He remembered the sun on his face and the wind in his hair. Each sip to his parched lips opened a forgotten door. The delicate grapes from the sun-kissed muscadine wine pressed their memories into him. He remembered for a moment. He smiled again. His eyes seemed to sparkle, if only for a moment. He clutched the bottle as she walked away and closed his eyes with a muscadine memory plucked from the vine.

About the author:

Sheila is at a ripened age of 50 and to her life is now like fine wine. She has been pressed through the years with stresses, sorrows, laughter and love. The good outweigh the bad and the memories are like the smooth, delicate flavor of muscadine wine lingering on her lips. Every day is a wonderful gift from God.

Sheila shares a tiny, cozy home in Ringgold, Georgia with her husband Hollis, Chihuahua Hoover and cat Tootie. From a previous marriage, she has three precious children, Zack, Laura, and Jake; and two adorable grandkids, Devin and James. She works fulltime as inventory management at Southeastern Salvage in Chattanooga, TN. She loves meeting people and discovering their personalities beginning with a simple smile. Her first book, *Sewn - a pioneer family saga*, she self-published online with Lulu Publishing. Sheila has several stories and books in progress. She loves bike riding and flea markets and spending time with family. She cherishes the autumn season. It's like love's arms are wrapped around her while watching the warm sun dip behind the mountains. It looks and feels like a glorious burst of heaven.

WINDOWS ON MILL STREET
©2011 by Kathleen Ratcliffe

"It's a beautiful day! It's a beautiful, glorious day! It is just a perfect day here on Mill Street!" Abigail gleefully surveyed the happy sights before her. The birds in the tree were singing as they diligently worked on their nest. It was spring at last and the avian family needed a good home. The young woman watched the birds flutter industriously in the branches. They worked together, singing all the while. "How sweet, they must be love birds." she exclaimed.

Suddenly, a powerful bang shook the building. Abigail pressed her nose to the window pane and, keeping it pressed to the glass, rotated her face left then right, drinking in the entire street. Seeing no cause for the din she continued to look at the city sights. Her eyes were as wide as a five-year-old's as she smiled at the hustle and bustle of the avenue. She took in all the actions of the pedestrians, surmising that each had a wonderful story to tell. While she longed to be a part of the goings-on, she treasured her view. Abigail loved to pick and choose which little saga to watch, adding her own theory of what was taking place.

The shop keeper who came out each day at this time was actually secretly in love with one of the women who passed by daily. Yes, there she was and ooh, he was watching her. Did she know? The object of his affection nodded indifferently as she passed by the rotund shop owner. The middle-aged woman on the corner searched every day in vain for her true love. She had not seen him since high school. Would she even recognize him all these years later? She dressed in her best attire just in case he came today. Three soldiers marched valiantly down the street as enamored women gazed, and captivated children tried to copy the confident stride of these men. Were they on their way to meet their wives? Perhaps the wives were three sisters waiting impatiently for their husbands to return from foreign travels.

Abigail stood back from the window, giggling at the print her nose had left. Opening her mouth wide she let out a huge breath onto the glass. Quickly she drew a heart with an arrow through it. Inside the heart she wrote:

RW
+
AW

She stared at it until the last of her rudimentary drawing had evaporated. Resuming her forgotten task, she reached into the bucket, found her cloth, and gave it a good wringing. Then she washed the window until it gleamed in the late afternoon sun. It was four-thirty. Not much longer until it would be five-fifteen—the most wonderful time of the entire day. Five-fifteen was when Robert would be home at last.

"Robert." She spoke his name aloud. The name purred from her lips. When she said his name, she said it as though no other name was worthy of her voice. There was no other in the entire world— just Robert.

He'd be coming soon. She looked down Mill Street. Soon she would see his now familiar gait. She knew it as soon as he came into view. Her heart would beat all the faster. The color would rise in her cheeks. Her eyes would see only him. He'd stop for a moment and wave to her before crossing Mill Street. Sometime she would spy him buying a bouquet of fragrant blooms. He'd brought her candy, fruit, and books. Once he saw an artist displaying his work and had purchased a landscape to hang on their parlor wall. No matter what, Robert always had a surprise for

Abigail.

They'd been married for only three months—three months, one week, and two days...four hours and twenty-five minutes! They had the most exquisite wedding ever. She'd always dreamed of a Christmas wedding. Robert moved heaven and earth to make her dreams come true. Everything had been perfection: the music, the candles, the red and green ribbons adorning the pews. The scent of pine wafting through the church had been heavenly. Instead of a bouquet, she carried a lovely white fur muff trimmed with a sprig of holly. Her dress was eggshell satin trimmed in butter cream velvet with a faint, raised paisley print discernable only on close inspection. Mother had gifted her with a forest green cape trimmed with white fur to keep her warm to and from the church.

But the most wonderful thing of all was marrying Robert. The event could have taken place in the middle of a corn field for all she cared. All had been flawless ever since.

Dutifully, Mother had taken Abigail aside the night before the wedding to tell her "about life". How wrong her mother had been: "Just lie there and close your eyes or look up at the ceiling. It will be over before you know it." It wasn't like that at all. Robert's touch thrilled her like nothing she'd ever imagined. His lips were soft and tender. She could kiss him all day and all night. When they were together, it was as though they melted together into one.

She closed her eyes and spun around, hugging herself. Catching a glimpse of herself in the mirror, she stopped. "Oh my, this will never do." She'd been so busy cooking, cleaning, and anticipating that she had forgotten to change. Flinging open the closet door she reached in and grabbed Robert's favorite, a pink floral dress with ivory collar and cuffs. He loved it on her not only because the color was pleasing, but it had all those buttons down the front. Buttons he could undo slowly while he gazed into her eyes and kissed her lips. They made love every night as soon as he got home. Made love before dinner and then again after dinner, sometimes all evening until sleep overtook their exhausted bodies. Yes, she performed her wifely duty. She smirked at this thought. Some duty! It was sheer bliss.

She hurried with her dressing and ran to her bureau to gather her mirror, brush, and pins. With great care she pinned her long brown hair up into a loose chignon. Abigail had dearly wanted to cut her long locks into one of the adorable bobs she'd seen, but when Robert begged her to leave her hair long, she happily complied. He loved to undo her hair, pulling the pins out, and stroking her hair as she chattered on about her day.

Abigail loved hearing about his day too. Robert was a newspaper man. He'd hoped soon to be an editor. He thought he'd be promoted this week. It had been between him and Theodore Hughes, but Robert had only been there for a year. He was already making a name for himself, but the boss explained that Theodore was next in line for advancement. It would come soon, he promised, but Abigail knew Robert was disappointed despite his claim to be relieved. He'd said there were other things out there for him; this might just help him find them.

It was a mistake not giving her husband the job, Abigail had thought. Robert knew everything. Every Sunday he mesmerized Abigail's parents with his tales from all over the world. He knew all the stories that were sent in from across the seas. He even knew some of the details that were left out.

One Sunday, Robert and Father had talked endlessly about the war in Europe. "There's no way President Wilson will get into that war. He promised that during the campaign," Father had adamantly exclaimed.

Robert had shaken his head, a knowing smile on his face. "Don't be so sure. Don't be so sure."

That's all she had heard of the conversation between her two favorite men. Mother had ushered her only child out of the dining room, requesting help with the dishes. "Women have no place speaking of politics or even listening," Mama admonished.

But it wasn't politics; it was that silly old war in a place far away. It was romantic hearing stories of foreign lands she'd never go to see.

There were still so many people still walking on Mill Street. Electricity could be felt in the air. Was it because it was almost time? As Abigail completed her grooming, she held the mirror up to her face and smiled. At last she was ready for Robert's arrival. Anxiously, Abigail looked up the street. She could feel her heart beat faster. He'd appear any minute. She laughed as she watched a soldier walking quickly up the street. A group of children marched merrily behind him. One even pretended to be playing a fife. She watched them come closer, and then the soldier stopped, looked up at the window and waved. Her heart pounded in her ears, her eyes bulged with shock. The hand mirror crashed to the floor as both hands flew up to her mouth.

The birds were chirping gaily outside in the big tree. The tree seemed close enough for William to touch. He pressed his whole body to the glass. "You building a new home, birdie, birdie, birdie?" the child questioned. He began to tap his fingers on the glass.

"Get away from that winda!" he heard Mrs. Blanchard yell. Then a loud noise made the building shake. He jumped, wondering what happened. Hesitantly, he backed away, then, realizing that the old woman had not caused the sudden sound, he went back to the glass.

He watched the people in the street for hours. The big man with the white apron had come out of his shop for a look. A lady passed by and nodded at the man. Would she go in to buy something? William wished he could go into the shop and look around. He wondered what was inside. Would it be anything he would want? What if there were toys in there and he could play for hours without being yelled at by Mrs. Blanchard!

Cars drove up and down the street. Every day, more cars were being driven. William wished for a car. He wanted to ride in one of them. He would honk the horn as loud as he could and wave at everyone he saw. Then he would find some friends and take them for a ride in the country. They could have a picnic and play games and swim in a pond.

Across the street he saw three boys walking with their mother. He watched them until they were out of sight. Where were they going? he wondered. He wished he had three brothers, or even one brother. He didn't want a sister, though. He had five girl cousins. They were mean and bossed him around.

William stared up at the sky. It was very blue and the clouds were fluffy. He didn't think it would be very much fun to sit around in a cloud all day. He wanted to play. He watched with envy as four boys ran down the street with a dog. The dog barked loudly at the boys who paid it no mind.

"I'll play with you, doggie!" William called, but the dog couldn't hear.

"Are you near that winda again?"

"No," William replied timidly. He stepped down from the window seat and looked at the grandfather clock which had just chimed once. The big hand was on the six and the little hand was on the four. That meant four-thirty. William's father had taught him how to tell time last year. Papa had been patient as he explained the clock. Now he never had to ask to be told the time. Mrs. Blanchard always grumbled when he had asked. Papa said she was a great cook and an even better housekeeper, but she was behind the door when personalities were given out. William didn't know what that meant but Papa laughed, so he did too.

Papa often got home at five o'clock (big hand on the twelve, little hand on the five), but sometimes he was too busy to leave work. William hoped today would be a five o'clock day. Papa was a doctor. He took care of sick people all day long. Some days they were really sick. Papa had said it was very important to take care of these people. He didn't want bad things to happen to them. That would make their families sad. He said sometimes the people would always be sick but at least their family still had them. He looked sad when he said that. William thought his father might cry, but he just hugged William.

This summer they would live in the country. Papa told William that the fresh air would be good for all of them. Every day there were more and more cars in the city. Heaven only knew what was in all that smoke that came from them. It couldn't be good to breathe in all that. Although William rarely went outside, he nodded when Papa said that. He listened expectantly as Papa told him about all the fun they would have in the country. There were lots of animals and fields and babbling brooks. There was a big pond maybe they could go in and cool off during the hot summer days. The house had a big porch that covered two sides. There was a swing on the porch. It was big enough that they could all sit on it at once. Papa promised to hang a swing from the oak tree branches in front of the house. That would be for William alone to use. Dreamily William thought about swinging higher and higher, up to the sky, up to the clouds.

Back to the window, he looked out again to the clouds. He and Papa had the highest apartment in the building. When they first came here Papa wanted to live in the ground floor so it would be easier for William to go out, but something happened and they moved here instead. The small boy had been happy. He liked to be up high.

From what he remembered, the ground floor apartment wasn't as big. There was no window seat in the parlor. He loved the comfy window seat. He could sit there and pretend all day.

Some solders had walked by again, he'd seen them earlier. "Bang, bang, bang." William aimed his finger at them.

"Get away from that winda, I tell ya!" Mrs. Blanchard had ears that could hear everything. Everything!

William moped away and sat in the corner where his wooden toys were kept neatly in the big red box. He pulled out the ship and the little boats. Then his eyes lit up. Tinker toys! Papa had built a windmill the other day. William wondered if he could make one as great as the one Papa made. He opened the can, turned it upside down, and spilled its contents on the floor. Expectantly, he looked up, prepared for the gruff voice of the housekeeper. Good, not this time, he thought. Playing for a few minutes, he lost interest and looked up at the clock. Big hand on the twelve, little hand on the five: five o'clock. William stared at the entrance hall, willing his father's appearance. Quietly, he waited. Hearing the door open and close several times in his mind, he slowed his breathing and smiled. Any second Papa would rush in and lift him up almost to the sky. Glancing back to the grandfather clock, he saw that the big hand had moved to the one. No, Papa would be late today. Somebody sick needed him.

That was alright. In a few minutes the nice man who always waved to him would be coming. William wasn't sure how he knew him or *if* he knew him. Maybe the man was just being friendly. He might know Papa. William meant to ask Papa if he knew the nice man but when his father came home on time William was so happy he forgot about everything else.

Back up to the window seat, William sat soundlessly, watching the people on Mill Street. It seemed busier than usual. More people were running about and talking to each other as they passed. What were they saying? Were they having fun? He looked back at the clock to see the big hand on the three. He looked down the street. No nice man today, instead a soldier waved to him. William waved back. "March, march, soldier."

"Get away from that winda!" Mrs. Blanchard's angry voice yelled.

"Blasted birds making all that racket!" Margaret glared out the window. Those creatures were at least four stories above her yet it sounded like they were right outside. Being down here at street level was awful. She missed her apartment on the top floor. All the noise from the street got on her nerves. Chatter, chatter, chatter, all day and half the night! If only she hadn't had to move. "Oh hang!" There were those birds singing their happy little song again. Margaret slammed the window down with such force that it seemed to shake the whole building. "Not *everyone* is happy," she scolded the birds.

Across the street she could make out the store owner standing in the shop doorway. Business must be bad. He's trying to lure customers as they pass by. A blur that must be a woman strolled by the shop. "That's it lady, keep going. He doesn't have anything you want."

Margaret's eyesight was getting worse every day. Most of what she was able to see came from memory. The same things happened out on Mill Street every day. Nothing changed. People said and did the same things as if by rote. The only thing that changed was her eyesight. *And this apartment*, Margaret thought. One day, unable to see the steps clearly, she nearly tripped and fell. That was when the landlord suggest Margaret move into the vacant apartment on the ground floor. She had resisted for a while then Doctor Harrison managed to talk her into the move. Doctor Harrison had been her doctor for many years. It was he who ruefully gave her the terrible prognosis.

The change seemed a good idea until Margaret learned that the good doctor was moving into her old apartment on the top floor. She thought perhaps he coaxed her to switch living quarters just so he and his sickly son could have her big, beautiful apartment. He probably wondered why she would want it anymore. Soon she wouldn't be able to see the lovely, large rooms. Their size would be difficult for her to negotiate with her limited vision. She'd no longer be able to appreciate the view from the big windows. Surely the doctor and his son would be better suited to that abode. How selfish of him to insist she relocate.

Months later, she overheard that it was not Doctor Harrison who finagled the move. On the contrary, he would have rather had the ground floor apartment as it was safer for his little boy. In fact, it was those church ladies on the second floor who suggested the thought to the landlord. This discovery made Margaret feel ashamed that she thought so poorly of Doctor Harrison. He'd been nothing but kind to her over the years. She couldn't apologize for snubbing him though as she'd have to confess to eavesdropping.

Ever since her sight started to fail, Margaret's other senses became stronger. Her hearing was especially keen. She could hear conversations quite clearly, even across the street. Sounds were more distinct now. She found she could perceive men's voices more readily than those of females. As a result, Margaret discovered herself regularly nosing in on the male banter. She heard them discuss the war in Europe. She knew about Funston, who had died two months ago. She loved the stories about "Black Jack." The overall opinion of these men was that the United States would enter the war soon. She heard the story of the Zimmermann telegram and how it was going to be the last straw. The progression to war was obvious from the headlines Margaret heard the newsboys shout each day.

How silly it was that women were not supposed to know anything about politics or war—or anything else for that matter. *Just keep us in the dark*, Margaret thought. *Look what happens. Your husband leaves, you end up blind, and in an apartment that you don't even like. Even people with good eyesight don't see what's really going on.*

Charles had left over fifteen years ago. At first her husband of ten years had told her he was going to travel about selling cleaning supplies. She could come with him if she liked, but he was going. That was final. Margaret didn't want to leave her mother and father, so she stayed behind. Charles came home once a month the first year, then less often after that. Then she saw him once a year. Now, she hadn't seen him in ten years. Not that she cared. Sadly, her parents had passed away over ten years ago. Mother had gotten the typhus and died. Her father died shortly after, surely from a broken heart.

Well, her heart would never be broken. Not by Charles, not by anyone else. She had plenty of money now. She didn't need anyone. Her mother had been right. Men only wanted one thing from their women; demanded one thing and it was just awful. She thought about the newlyweds who lived on the third floor. Margaret often heard them cooing and fawning. Why, it was enough to make her ill. That silly girl would learn all too soon not to believe any promise that man would make. Men were all like that, never living up to their word. Even the president had pledged to keep the country out of the war. Now it was going to happen any day. She'd heard the conversation outside her window just this morning. Well good, get rid of all the men. Send them all to Europe and let them be fodder for the Germans.

There were noticeably more soldiers on the street today. They were easier to make out from the other men. Even though she couldn't see clearly, Margaret was able to see how they seemed to march. Soon they would be on their way, never to return. Just like Charles.

Standing in front of her window now, she heaved a sigh. She could make out many people scurrying around on the street. Margaret could barely see a lone soldier on the other side. He seemed to be coming toward this building. A gloomy thought crossed her mind. What if that soldier was the husband of that silly young girl upstairs? How soon that child would learn what Margaret already knew. Despite herself, Margaret whispered a little prayer.

The sun shone brightly through the open window. Miriam opened one eye wearily, and then closed it again. The birds were busy outside in the tree. She couldn't see them, they were on one of the higher branches but she heard their gay song. She took a nice long stretch. It was warm here in the afternoon glow, just the thing for a nice long nap. Miriam sat up and looked out into the street. Lots was going on outside. Suddenly a loud thud shook the building. Surprised, Miriam arched her back, her fur standing on end, she waited motionlessly. No immediate danger. It was quiet in her domain. Satisfied that all was well, the contented cat began to lick her orange fur. Her rough tongue did its job; she then wet her paws well and used them to clean her face.

Time for a drink. Miriam pounced from the window seat to the chair and then to the floor where her water bowl sat. Just what she needed after a long snooze. A small unknown object was discovered under the table. Could this be a toy? Miriam wondered.

She batted it a few times with her paws but it didn't do anything exciting so she lost interest.

Back to the window, to the warmth, Miriam discovered the birds were flying close. If only she could get on the other side of this barrier. She stood on her hind legs and stretched her full length while leaning on the wooden sill. Her nails made ugly scraping noises on the glass, scaring the birds away. She caught a nail in the curtain and struggled for a minute before freeing herself. She ran to the big chair near the fireplace. It was the best thing in the house for nail sharpening. No one was around to hear the snapping and cracking. That done, Miriam found a small ball which she chased about for several minutes until it became tedious.

There was so much noise coming from the street. She leaped to her favorite place to quench her curiosity. Happy in the sun, Miriam sat watching the activity in the street below. She knew it wouldn't be much longer.

With that, the door opened. "Miriam, your Mamas are home," the sweet voiced one called. She'd be fed now, Miriam knew.

One of the ladies scooped Miriam up and talked happily to the cat. The other went about the business of getting food ready for the hungry feline.

"Virginia, did you see?" one of them asked. "Did you see that nice young man from upstairs? He had on an Army uniform?"

"He must have just joined." Virginia replied. "Mildred, we will have to look out for his sweet young bride."

Mildred nodded as she silently asked for Someone to look out for the young man.

About the author:
Kathleen was married on 10/10/10.

Kathleen Ratcliffe is a registered nurse whose career is divided between working clinically in a cardiac catherization laboratory and providing education to medical professionals all over the United States. Employed by a small company in Pennsylvania, her job involves composing educational material and instruction of the clinical aspects of invasive cardiology.

During the past fifteen years she became a single parent, studied to become a registered nurse and raised two children with the help of her wonderful mother. She then pursued a bachelor's degree while working to support her family. After years of writing papers and presentations related to nursing, she has been afforded the time to go back to writing fiction. Several stories are complete and others are in progress.

As sports editor for her high school paper, she attended a journalism seminar for high school editors at the Catholic University in Washington D.C. It was there where her fervor for writing expanded.

The proud mother of two children, her son is a PhD candidate in anthropology at Temple University. Her daughter is a student at Montgomery County Community College.

Besides writing, Kathleen's interests include running, cycling and yoga. Her husband, who is also a registered nurse, introduced her to the world of triathlon several years ago. Helping her conquer her fear of open water swimming, he made her realize that anything is possible if you try.

A CHANGE OF HEART
©2011 by Kenneth Corn

Dogs. Herbert Walker hated dogs. Well, Herb didn't hate the dogs *themselves*. He just hated having to take care of a dog. Herb cussed every time he had to brush dog hair off the couch after his pooch spent all day lounging there. He screamed obscenities while digging the dog crap from between the tread of his boots after stepping in a pile. But what Herb hated the most about owning a dog was when he found another empty bag of Dog Chow at feeding time. He couldn't stand the thought of spending twenty of his hard earned dollars every week on dog food. Such a waist of beer money!

So, why does Herb own a dog? That's a question he's been asking himself ever since Gracie came into his life. If Herb had been man enough to stand up to his nine-year-old daughter, he may have been spared from the responsibilities of being a dog owner. But, as Herb's ex-wife told him over and over, "You let your daughter walk all over you." Herb would rather gouge his eyeballs out with a fork than admit she was right.

Herb divorced his wife a little over a year ago. When he moved out of their two story suburban palace, he searched for the cheapest place he could find to lay his head at night. Between a low paying job and the ridiculously high child support, money for rent was scarce.

During the search for his new bachelor pad, Herb discovered that a mortgage payment for a ranch-style house on the shady side of town was cheaper than renting an apartment in one of those complexes with a clubhouse and pool. He paid less a month and built equity. A win-win situation. Herb really didn't care if his next-door neighbor was selling pharmaceuticals at the end of his driveway. As long as he didn't try to sell Herb a Baggie of pure pleasure, he didn't see why they couldn't coexist.

Now that Herb had his own place, his daughter could spend the night every other weekend. The first time his ex-wife saw the house, she refused to let her baby stay. Herb couldn't imagine why his ex was worried about her only child staying here in what the local news labeled as "the most dangerous neighborhood in the city." What could Herb do to change the old hag's mind?

With one of those little octagon-shaped yard signs stuck in his overgrown flowerbed, Herb tricked his ex-wife into believing he had installed an alarm system. Instead of opening up his wallet for some useless electronics, Herb had driven around the neighborhood looking for an empty house for sale. When he found one, he stole the ADT sign out of the yard. Herb figured an empty house didn't really need a sign to discourage burglars.

Herbert did spend some serious money on home security though. At the local gun shop, he found a bargain on a Smith and Wesson .44 Special. Since Herb had never owned a gun before, he signed up for some shooting lessons. When Herb had the gun in his hands, he felt no fear. *The gangbangers better stay away,* Herb thought as he fondled the weapon, *because I won't hesitate to pop a cap in their ass.*

Later, after spending an afternoon at the shooting range, Herb thought about how the punks around his house probably carried heavier artillery than a handgun. His little cap gun wouldn't be very effective against a Kalashnikov. Maybe he should have bought the Mossberg pistol grip shotgun. But, it's kind of hard to stuff one of those in the waistband of your jeans when you want to carry it out in your yard to check on a strange noise.

The previous owners of this slice of paradise Herb now owned had walled off the boundary of the back yard with a five-foot high chain link fence. A thin trail of bare dirt ran along the edge of the fence. When he looked at the path cut in the grass, he imagined a soldier with a rifle propped up on his shoulder, pacing back and forth along the barrier. Another thin trail of bare dirt ran from the back doorstep out to a decrepit doghouse. It was in such bad shape, Herb supposed one huff and puff from the big bad wolf would blow it away. Waterlogged pressboard, splitting around the edges, covered the walls and a sheet of rusty corrugated metal topped off the mess.

When Herb's daughter saw the pitiful doghouse, she said, "Daddy, you have the perfect place for my new dog."

"What?" Herb ripped his attention away from the TV to see her standing in front of the sliding glass door. She had her back turned to him and was staring out at the back yard while she talked.

"Dad, a dog would keep you company when I'm not here."

"I don't have the time or the patience to deal with a dog."

"And a dog would be the perfect playmate for me when I am here."

"Yes, but..."

"Did you know that houses with dogs are less likely to be broken into?"

"How do you know that?"

"I read it in one of my library books about dogs."

Clearly, having a dog is a constant thought in her mind, Herb thought as he eyed his little princess standing in the dining room. He knew his baby's mother would never allow an animal to roam the pristine halls of her suburban palace. Maybe this could be an opportunity for Herb to earn some daddy points and piss off the old lady at the same time. The first time Herb's daughter went with dog crap on her shoes, her mother would probably throw the contaminated Skechers in the garbage. Then she would call Herb demanding he buy a new pair of e-overpriced sneakers. Herb couldn't wait for the moment he could yell "No!" at his ex-wife and pop his cell phone shut on her ear.

A smile spread over Herb's face at this last thought. "How

would you like to go to the animal shelter today?"

She turned from the sliding glass door with a huge grin and ran toward Herb. He barely had enough time to tense his muscles before she leapt over the side of the recliner and landed in his lap. Score one for Big Daddy!

That afternoon Herb met his worst nightmare. His daughter picked out the largest dog she could find begging for her affection through a chain link gate at the pound. The shelter volunteer told Herb she believed the dog was a mix between a Boxer and a Great Dane. Herb groaned at the thought of all the food this monster would consume on a daily bases. Then his mind wandered to the question of how much crap this mutt would deposit in his yard. Why such a big dog? Why couldn't he put his foot down and tell Princess she had to pick out a smaller money pit. Herb suddenly felt like banging his head on the metal support column next to him.

"Dad, I'm going to name her Gracie."

What a fitting name for such a hoss of a dog, Herb thought.

The dog lived up to Herb's expectations and then some. It sucked the dog food out of its bowl as if it were a vacuum cleaner. Herb wanted to name the damn thing "Hoover" instead of the cutesy name his daughter had bestowed upon the mutt. In a matter of two weeks, the back yard became a minefield saturated with dog bombs. Herb's daughter was supposed to eliminate the poop hiding in the grass on the weekends when she came to visit. But, the bottom of Herb's boots after mowing revealed that there was a pronounced misunderstanding in the rules he had discussed with her.

Herb had anticipated the inconveniences of feeding and cleaning up dog shit. But he was not prepared for the buckets of black hair the Hoover shed all over the house. Gobs of black strands formed a nest on the couch where Gracie lounged. No matter how often he vacuumed the floor, the hair seemed to grow out of the carpet as if it were grass. Herb wanted to keep the dog outside but his daughter protested. She won that argument by informing her daddy that it was inhumane to leave Gracie outside in the ninety-degree heat.

"The back yard doesn't even have a single tree to shade Gracie from the burning sun," she pleaded.

"What about the dog house?"

"Dad," she rolled her eyes. "I bet it's hotter in the dog house than out in the yard."

Daughter wins again. From then on, the dog had the run of the house.

One evening when Gracie was sprawled out on the couch and Herb was channel surfing, Gracie suddenly lifted her head to look at the front door. Her ears stood up in sharp points on her meaty head and her nose wiggled back and forth as she inspected the air.

"Gracie," Herb said. "What's the matter, girl?"

Gracie shot from the couch as if she'd been fired from a cannon. She began to jump up against the door as if she were trying to bust the door down. Herb heaved himself out of the chair and walked over to her. He was about to grab her by her collar when he decided to take a peek out of the small diamond shaped window in the door. He figured a stray dog from the neighborhood had picked up Gracie's scent and came up on to the porch to investigate.

Herb's eyes widened to the size of silver dollars as he looked across the yard to the street. A strange car sat in front of the house and three hooded shapes where jogging up the cement walkway leading to the porch.

"Oh, shit!" Herb screamed when he noticed long tubular shadows strongly resembling gun barrels protruding from their hands. Adrenalin surged through his body as if someone had jammed a syringe into his neck and injected it straight into his bloodstream.

Herb spun on his heels and bolted through the house as if he were the Six Million Dollar Man. Gracie followed him. The crash of his front door exploding inward reached his ears as he crossed the threshold of his bedroom. He dove for his .44 Special sitting on top of the nightstand next to his bed. One of his outstretched arms knocked the reading lamp off the table as he scooped the pistol into his arms. The lamp shattered on the floor.

Once Herb had the weapon in his hands, he got up and returned to the bedroom door, slamming it shut. He flipped the lock on the doorknob, knowing this door offered much less protection than the solid wood front door the assailants just shattered. But at this point he was only reacting rather than thinking about what the hell he was doing.

Gracie crouched down on her back legs as if she were a snake ready to strike. She emitted a low guttural growl from between her bared teeth as she and Herb listened to heavy footsteps thump down the hallway.

"Don't come in here," Herb yelled through the door. "I've got a gun."

The thug leading the invasion must not have cleaned the wax out of his ears before coming on this little adventure. Despite Herb's warning, the thief grabbed the knob on the other side and began twisting it back and forth. Fear took control over Herb's brain, telling him not to wait for this guy to give the door a hard kick. Herb knew if he let the intruder get past this door, the thug would spray the room with bullets in an attempt to eliminate any threats. Herb took a step back and leveled the business end of his revolver at the center of the door.

The first boom of the gun firing was deafening in the tiny bedroom. Gracie's growls turned to howls of pain at the piercing sound. Herb's ears rang as if he just spent two hours at a Van Halen concert. The sudden shock to Herb's auditory senses caused him to hesitate for a moment. What was he doing just pulling the trigger like that? An unfamiliar voice shouting at him through the new door hole brought Herb back to the crisis at hand. He immediately pulled the trigger again.

This time he shot twice, hoping like hell one of the bullets found something fleshy to bore into. Herb stopped after the third shot, thinking he needed to save the remaining bullets for the other two intruders in case they decided to try coming into his room.

Herb heard a cry of pain as shouts drowned out the ringing in his ears and Gracie's howling. He kept the gun leveled at the door ready to fire again if it moved so much as a millimeter. Gracie's howls reverted back to growls as she started flinging herself against the flimsy bedroom door. Her attack made it difficult to hear what was happening in the hallway. The shouts and cries of pain seemed to be fading but Herb couldn't tell for sure. At some point, he was going to have to open the door to face whoever decided his house was a good target for pillaging. But if he opened the door Gracie would charge through, becoming a target.

Wait a minute. Was he really worried about the dog getting hurt? Gracie had been a pain in his ass since the day he brought her home. All the hair throughout the house. All the crap in the yard. But she had just saved his life. If Gracie weren't a part of his life, he would have been sitting in his recliner when the thugs broke down the door. He wouldn't have made it to his gun. For all he knew, he might be sprawled out on his living room floor, bleeding from multiple bullet wounds. He was alive because of the damn dog.

Herb couldn't figure out what to do. He thought he had the thugs on the run but he was genuinely concerned for Gracie's safety. While pondering this sudden dilemma, Herb realized he wasn't hearing any screaming in the hallway any more. Had the invaders left the house?

Finally, Herb jerked the door open. Gracie charged down the hallway and was in the living room before Herb even stepped through the door. Before Herb could run halfway down the hall, he heard a blood-curdling scream of pain from outside. Gracie must have caught up with the bad guys in the yard.

Herb reached the front door to see the same three shapes he saw earlier retreating back to the parked car in the street. This time they looked like a band of wounded soldiers running for their lives. The one Herb shot had his arm draped over another's shoulder, using him for support. The third thug was stumbling around in a circle, trying to shake Gracie off his pant leg.

Scared that the guy might shoot Gracie, Herb brought up his pistol and aimed. The dude managed to shake Gracie off by continuously kicking her with his free leg. Gracie fell back with a whimper and the thug sprinted to the car. Herb nearly pulled the trigger when he saw Gracie hit the ground. But, she was up and charging again before he could shoot. The other two hoodlums piled into the backseat, shouting wildly as Gracie bit at their heels. The car's engine roared to life and sped off in a shower of loose gravel kicked up by the spinning tires.

Herb dropped to one knee and laid his gun on the grass. Gracie chased the car for a few yards then turned back to see Herb kneeling in the yard. She seemed to glide on air as she raced toward him.

"Good girl," Herb shouted as Gracie crashed into his outstretched arms. Her tongue felt hot and wet on his face as she showered him with doggie kisses. Herb stroked her from head to tail with both hands. After tonight he knew that he would be giving her much more love and attention. She had saved his life.

Gracie rolled over on her back, which Herb always thought meant she wanted him to scratch her belly. He has since learned that when a dog rolls over on its back it is a sign of trust. Nowadays, Herb feels more than trust for his four-legged companion. He loves Gracie more than any other living being in his life—except for his baby girl, of course.

Herb may still dislike dogs, but to him Gracie isn't a dog. She is family.

About the author:

Kenneth Corn is a photojournalist for a local NBC affiliate in Charlotte, North Carolina. After fourteen years of witnessing many news events through the lens of his camera, Kenneth started writing short stories based on his experiences. He has contributed several articles to his television station's website giving readers a behind the scenes look at how reporters and photographers cover the news. Other writing credits include publishing an article in News Photographer magazine about being an embedded photojournalist during Operation Iraqi Freedom.

THE WALL SHADOW
©2011 by Mary Smith

Maggie thought she heard a noise in her room and mentally cursed, thinking, *There goes a good night's sleep again.* Lately she had been getting up to use the bathroom several times a night because, at seventy years old, her bladder wasn't what it used to be. But this time it sounded like rats with their sharp little nails scurrying across the wood floor or behind the walls. She raised her head and prepared to throw back the covers from her body when her attention was drawn to the wall opposite her bed. There, in silhouette amongst the flowered wallpaper, was a shadow of a person—or what resembled a person—that seemed to be sitting on nothing, but crouched as though reclining.

A breeze kicked up outside, making the lower branches of the oak just outside her bedroom scrape against the side of the house. As the tree moved, so did the shadow, and just as she was about to laugh at herself for being so foolish, the image on the wall spoke to her.

"Good evening." The voice was whispery and had no tones of man or woman. "How are you tonight?" it asked.

At first, Maggie couldn't speak, not so much from fear as just plain shock. She finally managed to blurt out, "Who the hell are you?"

"I'm no one." The image moved slightly with the wind outside but stayed on the wall. "I've just come to keep you company through this night. It's going to be a long one, after all."

"What do you mean a long one?" Maggie demanded.

The image ignored her question, instead saying, "I will start by telling stories from your past, how's that?" Without waiting for a reply, the voice began telling tales of Maggie's childhood and her exploits later in life.

By the time the thing was nearly to her old age years, Maggie began to feel the tug of her bladder again. "Hey you," she said sleepily to her shadow friend, "I need to hit the bathroom, so can you get to a stopping place pretty quick?"

"Go ahead," the figure responded, "I'll just speak a little louder so you can hear."

How the hell is it gonna whisper any louder? Maggie thought as she threw back the covers and slung her legs over the sides of the bed. The shadow kept speaking as Maggie pushed her feet into her old fuzzy slippers; and when she had her robe wrapped securely around her wide girth, she headed for the bathroom that was just off the bedroom. Mentally, she thanked her long dead husband for insisting on a bathroom in the bedroom although she had been dead set against it at the time. Now in her old age, and with her body quitting on her as it was, she knew the idea had been a foresighted one. She could hear the whispery voice behind her as she shuffled into the bathroom and began to pull the door shut behind her.

"Please," the voice said, "leave the door open. I can't see anything—and wouldn't look if I could—but you will be able to hear much better."

Grumbling under her breath, Maggie shoved the door open again and began to take off the robe so she could sit on the commode. *No sense creating any more laundry than necessary,* she thought.

As she was about to sit, Maggie felt something underneath her foot and, forgetting she was old, fat, and over-balanced easily, she raised her foot again to see what she stepped on. She began to teeter, and when she tried to counteract the coming fall, she overdid that, too, and went down. Her head struck the commode first, bounced, and then smacked against the tile floor of the bathroom. She felt it as both hips cracked under her weight, and within just a few seconds she didn't feel anything as she faded into unconsciousness, and very shortly into death caused by the swelling of her injured brain.

The shadow on the bedroom wall quickly finished its story with the words, "And she lay in the bathroom on the floor until the next day when the home health caregiver came to take care of her and found her lifeless body."

And now the being is on its way to the local nursing home to see a Mrs. Wright, who is waiting to hear about *her* life, although she doesn't know it yet.

About the author:

Mary is an apartment-complex manager for the elderly and disabled or handicapped. She has been doing this for the last five years and had put her writing to the side for a very long time. Now she is a single (close to elderly) individual and suddenly can spend time pursuing the craft anew. She hopes that someone reads and gets some enjoyment out of her work as she writes what strikes her at the moment. She asks that you be patient since she feels as though she is starting over in high school again.

www.ingramcontent.com/pod-product-compliance
Lightning Source LLC
Chambersburg PA
CBHW051252170626
46809CB00004B/1612